Corvina
Sweeney

I0694970

WARNING

Reading this book may cause uncontrollable outbursts of laughter, which is temporary. It can also cause the urge to finger gun family, friends, and even strangers. This condition can become permanent and there is no known treatment

THE COVEN

CORVINA SWEENEY

LAUDANUM + LACE PUBLISHING

Paperback ISBN: 978-1-966692-10-2

Copyright © 2025 by Corvina Sweeney and Laudanum and Lace

Publishing

All rights reserved.

No portion of this book may be reproduced in any form without

written permission from the publisher or author, except as permit-

ted by U.S. copyright law.

To my ever-loving and *mostly* supportive husband—who has somehow survived my late-night writing marathons, endless book ideas, and occasional cackling at my own jokes. You deserve an award (or at least a really strong drink).

And to the **Sisters of the Sacred Moon Coven**—for the magic, the mischief, and the unwavering belief that every problem can be solved with a well-placed spell, a glass of wine, or a good old-fashioned hex.

May this book bring you laughter, chaos, and just the right amount of witchery.

CONTENTS

CHAPTER 1

Albany, Louisiana is a small quaint farming town just north of New Orleans in the lower part of the Bible Belt. The town itself isn't really much of a town. It consists of a handful of streets inside town limits with a single traffic light. The center of town consists of a couple of gas stations, a post office, Ruby's Diner, a hardware store, grocery store, a church, and the main attraction: a McDonald's that everyone seems to grumble about. Outside of town limits, there are multiple subdivisions and a Dollar General. Most of the older neighborhoods outside of town are heavily wooded, with the residents there owning acreage and cattle pastures.

The town folk are generally nice, usually making outsiders feel welcome. The people there go to the same schools from kindergarten to high school. The majority never leave the town. Like most small towns, Albany is close-knit, and everyone seems to be related by either blood or marriage.

To an outsider, it's quite the adjustment, especially if you're a woman, the men in town can be a bit... *old-fashioned.* Walk into the barbershop, and the conversation dies mid-sentence, every head turning like you've just walked in wearing a ballgown and combat boots. They go back to their business, but only once you leave. The same thing happens at Ruby's Diner, where the older men gather for their evening coffee and political discussions. It's not that they're outright rude—they just don't seem to know what to do with a woman who isn't pouring their coffee or nodding along to their opinions.

It's that *deep South, set-in-their-ways kind of thing,* where a man's word is final, and women are expected to keep to their own circles. You'd think with attitudes like that, half of them would have never gotten married—but then again, maybe that's why they spend all their time at the diner in the first place.

That's why when the word of a coven got around town, the townsfolk started gossiping and speculating on who they could be. Talk of devil worshipping was on the lips of every church-going local. The town was in a frenzy, and the tension was so thick in the air, any false step could send the townsfolk running for their torches and pitchforks.

The old Victorian mansion stood silently in the woods about a mile outside of town. Its facade showed its age with its weathered cypress boards and its faded, peeling paint. The windows stared out like old, dark eyes, remembering the lives that once walked its old hallways and the laughter that echoed through every room. The sprawling grounds were slightly overgrown, its ancient flower beds overtaken by weeds and neglect. The woods surrounding the property were old and filled with a mixture of ancient oaks and pine trees. Along the sides of the house stood old camellias that were in full bloom, and the back and front yards were dotted with the occasional crepe myrtle. Old, overgrown gardenia bushes lined the front of the home.

"Those will need to be cleaned up and trimmed," Emmaline said to the recently hired groundskeeper, as she pointed toward the gardenia bushes.

The groundskeeper, a wiry man in his late fifties with sun-weathered skin and a perpetual scowl, nodded curtly. "Yes, ma'am," he said, his voice gravelly from years of chain-smoking and, Emmaline suspected, cursing at weeds. He adjusted his frayed baseball cap, eyeing the overgrown gardenia bushes as if they were personally responsible for all his troubles. "This place'll take more than a week, though. Ain't been touched in decades. Probably haunted, too."

Emmaline's green eyes sparkled with mischief. "Oh, definitely haunted," she said lightly. "By a ghost who hates excuses. Think about that while you're trimming."

The man gave her a sharp look, unsure whether she was joking or serious, before muttering something unintelligible and trudging off toward the bushes. Emmaline watched him go, a smirk tugging at her lips. She turned back to the house, her gaze sweeping over the weathered facade and peeling paint.

"Definitely haunted," she murmured under her breath, this time to herself. But it wasn't the ghosts of former residents that worried her. It was the living, breathing townsfolk of Albany and their insatiable appetite for gossip.

Inside, the house greeted her with its usual mix of grandeur and mild chaos. The grand staircase, though dust-covered and creaky, still managed to exude a certain defiant elegance. The stained-glass window on the landing cast shifting patterns of color on the hardwood floor, and the faint scent of old wood and forgotten memories filled the air.

"Are we ever going to sweep this floor, or are we embracing the whole 'witches in a spooky mansion' stereotype?" a voice called from the parlor. Emmaline rolled her eyes and stepped into the room, where her best friend Moira was lounging on a velvet armchair with a glass of wine.

Moira, with her wavy brunette hair and penchant for dramatic flair, fit right into the aesthetic of the old Victorian house. She held up her wineglass in a mock toast. "To peeling paint, suspicious townsfolk, and mysterious floorboard creaks!"

Emmaline snorted. "The groundskeeper thinks the place is haunted."

"Of course he does. This house *looks* haunted. Did you tell him about the pentagram in the attic yet?"

"Shut up," Emmaline said, laughing. "We don't need the entire town breaking down the door with torches and pitchforks."

"Fair point," Moira said, swirling her wine. "So, how's our little coven of outcasts doing today?"

As if on cue, the front door banged open, and a third voice rang out. "Ladies, I have acquired provisions!"

They both turned to see Kirsten, arms full of grocery bags and an expression of triumph on her face. She was the practical one of the group, with short blonde hair and a no-nonsense attitude that balanced Moira's theatrics and Emmaline's dry humor.

"Provisions?" Emmaline asked, raising an eyebrow.

"Snacks, wine, and sage," Kirsten replied. "You know, the essentials."

"Ah, yes, sage," Moira said with mock seriousness. "For clearing out all the negative energy. Or for seasoning chicken."

Kirsten set the bags down on the dusty coffee table and shot Moira a look. "I swear, if you don't start helping me clean this place—"

"Relax," Moira said, grinning. "I'm supervising."

Kirsten rolled her eyes and pulled out a bundle of sage. "I'm burning this as soon as the groundskeeper leaves. That man has bad vibes."

"Agreed," Emmaline said, flopping onto the couch. "He keeps looking at me like I'm hiding the devil in the pantry."

"Well, technically—" Moira started, but Emmaline cut her off with a throw pillow to the face.

They laughed, the sound echoing through the old house. For all its quirks, the mansion already felt like home. Sure, the townsfolk were suspicious, and the house seemed to groan and creak more than was strictly necessary, but the three of them were used to being the subject of speculation. They'd been called worse than witches in their time, and frankly, they found the whole thing more entertaining than threatening.

Still, as Emmaline leaned back and stared up at the cracked plaster ceiling, she couldn't shake the feeling that the house *was* watching them. Not in a menacing way, exactly, but in the way an old dog might keep an eye on its new owners, curious and a little skeptical. Whatever secrets the house held, they'd unravel them in time—and probably over several bottles of wine.

For now, though, there were gardenias to trim, sage to burn, and a very skeptical groundskeeper to keep on his toes.

CHAPTER 2

The living room was a mess. Emmaline stood in the center of the chaos, hands on her hips, surveying the scene with a mixture of determination and despair. Dust blanketed every surface, cobwebs hung like ghostly decorations from the corners of the ceiling, and the faint, mysterious smell of mildew seemed to linger no matter how many windows they opened. A massive, sagging couch occupied one wall, its upholstery torn in several places, revealing yellowed stuffing beneath.

"This is what we get for buying a house sight unseen," Kirsten muttered, tugging on a pair of bright yellow cleaning gloves and kicking an overturned box out of her way.

"We didn't buy it," Moira pointed out from her perch on the rickety staircase. She was halfway through a can of soda and had done absolutely no cleaning so far. "We inherited it. From a relative none of us knew existed."

"Yeah, a distant, probably cursed relative," Kirsten shot back, snapping her gloves for emphasis. "Which is why we're here cleaning up this disaster instead of, you know, enjoying our Saturday."

Emmaline crouched to inspect a broken lampshade, brushing away a thick layer of grime. "I think it has charm," she said optimistically. "A little love and elbow grease, and it'll feel like home."

"It feels like tetanus," Kirsten said, scowling at the state of the floorboards. "Do you think this place has termites?"

Moira shrugged. "If it does, they're probably the only thing holding it together."

"Thanks for the support," Emmaline said dryly, tossing the lampshade into a garbage bag.

Kirsten straightened, her short blonde hair damp with sweat from her half-hearted scrubbing. "I'm just saying, this whole 'mysterious house in the woods' thing is giving me *very* haunted vibes."

"It's not haunted," Emmaline replied automatically, though she couldn't deny the uneasy feeling she'd had since they arrived. The house did have a presence about it—something watchful, as though the walls themselves were listening. But she chalked it up to her imagination and the natural creaks of an old building settling.

"Besides," she added, brushing her hands on her jeans, "even if it *were* haunted, we're witches. Shouldn't we be the ones haunting other people?"

Moira snickered. "She has a point."

"You're both delusional," Kirsten muttered, wiping her forehead with the back of her hand. "This place is falling apart, and we don't even have a functioning kitchen yet. How are we supposed to cook spells—or, you know, *food*?"

"Who needs a functioning kitchen when we have takeout?" Moira asked, grinning.

"Do you really think a pizza place delivers this far out in the sticks?" Kirsten shot back, waving toward the window. Beyond the overgrown yard, the thick woods stretched out in all directions, their shadows deepening as the sun sank lower in the sky.

"We can try," Moira said. "What's life without a little risk?"

"Speaking of risk," Emmaline interjected, changing the subject, "has anyone seen the groundskeeper lately?"

Kirsten frowned. "He was hacking at those gardenia bushes this morning. Haven't seen him since."

Moira shrugged. "Maybe he quit. Can't blame him, really. I wouldn't want to work for us either."

"Well, if he *did* quit, we're going to have to finish the yard ourselves," Emmaline said, wincing at the thought. "It's bad enough inside; we don't need the outside looking like something out of a horror movie."

"Speaking of horror movies," Moira said, hopping down from the staircase, "when are we meeting the locals? Isn't that, like, step one in moving to a creepy small town? Introduce yourselves, let everyone size you up, and figure out who the potential mob leaders are?"

Emmaline sighed. "We'll meet them eventually. We've been here all of two days. Let's focus on cleaning up the house first."

"And not dying of whatever lung disease lives in this dust," Kirsten added, coughing dramatically.

The three of them worked in relative silence for the next hour, tackling the worst of the grime in the living room. Emmaline scrubbed the fireplace mantle, uncovering intricate carvings beneath the layers of soot and dirt. Kirsten attacked the windows with vinegar and newspaper, muttering under her breath about the futility of it all. Moira, after much cajoling, finally picked up a broom and halfheartedly swept the floor, leaving small piles of dust in her wake.

By the time the sun dipped below the horizon, the room was marginally cleaner, though still far from presentable. The air was cooler now, carrying the faint scent of jasmine from the overgrown bushes outside. Emmaline lit a few candles, their warm glow softening the harsh edges of the room.

"Not bad," she said, stepping back to admire their progress. "It's starting to feel... almost livable."

Kirsten flopped onto the sagging couch, pulling off her gloves with a sigh. "Livable is a stretch, but at least I don't feel like I'm going to catch something just by breathing."

Moira plopped down beside her, grabbing a bag of chips from one of their supply boxes. "So," she said, between bites, "what's the plan tomorrow? More cleaning? Or do we start exploring the town and scaring the locals?"

Emmaline sank into a battered armchair, exhaustion tugging at her limbs. "Let's see how much we can get done here first. Then maybe we'll venture into town

Outside, the woods were alive with the hum of crickets and the occasional hoot of an owl. The house, though still rough around the edges, felt a little less daunting now, as though it were warming to its new inhabitants.

But as the laughter faded and the candles burned lower, Emmaline couldn't shake the feeling that something—or someone—was watching them.

She glanced toward the window, half expecting to see the groundskeeper lurking in the shadows. But there was nothing there—only the dense woods and the faint flicker of fireflies.

"Probably just my imagination," she murmured to herself, shaking off the unease.

Still, she couldn't help but wonder what secrets the house—and the town—might be hiding.

CHAPTER 3

By the time the morning sun poured through the cracked and dusty windows, the witches were already back at work. Dust motes swirled lazily in the beams of light, giving the room a golden, almost serene quality that belied the state of chaos they were still dealing with.

Kirsten balanced precariously on a wobbly stepladder, attacking a particularly stubborn cobweb in the corner of the dining room ceiling. "I don't even think this is dust anymore," she muttered, scrubbing furiously with a damp rag. "I think it's evolved into a sentient life form."

"Try talking to it," Moira called from across the room, where she was half-heartedly sweeping. "Maybe it'll pack its bags and leave."

"If I fall off this ladder, I'm haunting you first," Kirsten shot back, wobbling slightly.

Emmaline sat cross-legged on the floor, her sleeves rolled up as she polished one of the old wooden chairs they'd uncovered the day before. "At least it's not *that* bad," she said, squinting at the streaks of grime left behind on the wood. "We've seen worse."

"Yeah, in horror movies," Moira quipped. She paused mid-sweep to inspect a cracked floorboard. "Do you think this is structurally sound, or is this the kind of house where the floor collapses dramatically if we argue too loudly?"

"It's fine," Emmaline replied, though her tone wasn't entirely confident. "Mostly fine."

Kirsten snorted from her perch. "Mostly fine is not reassuring."

Before Emmaline could respond, there was a sharp knock at the front door. The sound echoed through the house, cutting through the hum of their banter. They froze, exchanging glances.

"Groundskeeper," Emmaline guessed, setting down her cloth. She rose to her feet and dusted off her hands. "I'll get it."

She opened the door to find Joe Wilkes standing there, his familiar scowl firmly in place. He wore the same frayed baseball cap as the day before, and his posture suggested he'd rather be anywhere else. Beside him stood two younger men, each holding shovels and looking slightly less miserable than Joe.

"Morning," Joe said gruffly, tipping his cap. "Brought some help today."

Emmaline stepped aside, her curiosity piqued. "Good morning. Who've you got with you?"

Joe gestured to the taller of the two, a lanky young man with sandy blond hair and a faint smattering of freckles. "This here's Jeremy, my brother's boy."

Jeremy gave a halfhearted nod, his eyes flicking around the entryway as if cataloging everything that was wrong with the house. He looked to be about nineteen, with the kind of perpetual slouch that suggested he was either always tired or allergic to effort.

"And this one's Clay," Joe continued, motioning to the stockier young man beside him. Clay had dark hair that curled slightly at the ends and a face that seemed permanently smudged with dirt, though his easy grin suggested he didn't mind. He looked to be in his early twenties, his broad shoulders and calloused hands hinting at a life spent doing hard labor.

"Nice to meet you both," Emmaline said, offering a smile. "Thanks for coming out to help."

Clay nodded politely. "Yes, ma'am. Uncle Joe said y'all had a lot to clean up."

"That's putting it lightly," Moira called from the dining room, sticking her head out into the hall. "You got a flamethrower in that truck of yours?"

Joe ignored her, stepping inside with a critical glance around the entryway. "We'll start with the bushes out front," he said. "Maybe tackle the back later, if there's time."

"Sounds like a plan," Emmaline said. "Let me know if you need anything."

Jeremy sighed loudly. "Yeah, like a nap."

"Jeremy," Joe barked, his tone sharp enough to make the younger man straighten. "You can nap when the work's done."

Jeremy muttered something under his breath but followed Clay out the door without further complaint.

Moira leaned against the wall, watching them go. "I like the big one," she said, smirking. "Seems like he has a good attitude."

Emmaline rolled her eyes. "Be nice. They're here to help."

By mid-afternoon, the dining room was looking almost respectable. Kirsten had managed to clear most of the cobwebs, though her arms ached from the effort, and Emmaline had polished the last of the wooden chairs. Even Moira, who had spent most of the morning making sarcastic comments, had contributed by sweeping the floor and wiping down the windowsills.

The sound of hedge trimmers and shovels filtered in from the yard, punctuated by the occasional burst of laughter from Clay and Jeremy. Joe, true to form, was silent as he worked, though his nephews seemed to find ways to amuse themselves, despite Joe's gruff demeanor.

"They're making progress out there," Emmaline said, peering through the window. Clay was trimming one of the overgrown gardenias, his movements efficient and precise, while Jeremy leaned on his shovel, clearly taking his time.

"I'd pay good money to know what they're talking about," Moira said, joining her at the window. "Think Joe's yelling at them?"

"Probably," Emmaline replied with a grin.

Kirsten dropped onto the newly cleaned couch with a sigh, pulling off her gloves. "Alright, we've earned a break. Who's up for a trip into town?"

"Do we have to?" Moira whined. "Town means people."

"And groceries," Kirsten countered. "Unless you want to live on cookies and boxed wine forever."

Moira perked up. "That doesn't sound so bad."

"Groceries it is," Emmaline interjected, grabbing her keys. "Let's go before I change my mind."

The drive into Albany was short but felt like stepping into another world. The town's single traffic light blinked lazily as they pulled onto Main Street, passing a row of modest brick buildings that housed the hardware store, pharmacy, and post office.

They parked in front of the grocery store, a squat, weathered building with a hand-painted sign that read *Patterson's Groceries*. Inside, the air was cool and smelled faintly of lemons and old wood.

The cashier, a stout woman with sharp eyes and a name tag that read *Mabel*, greeted them with a curt nod as they entered. Her gaze lingered on them for a moment, curiosity evident in the way she adjusted her glasses.

"You ladies new in town?" she asked as they approached the produce section.

Emmaline nodded. "Just moved into the old Pritchard place."

Mabel's eyebrows shot up. "The Pritchard place? Well, I'll be. Thought that house'd never see another family."

"It's a work in progress," Emmaline said diplomatically.

Mabel chuckled. "That's one way to put it." She leaned a little closer, lowering her voice. "You take care out there, alright? That place has... history."

"Doesn't everything in this town?" Moira quipped, earning a sharp elbow from Kirsten.

Mabel smiled faintly but didn't elaborate. Instead, she handed them their receipt with a final piece of advice. "We've got Sunday service at St. Mark's this weekend, if you're interested. Starts at nine. You're more than welcome."

Emmaline smiled politely. "Thanks. We'll think about it."

As they loaded the groceries into the car, Moira shook her head. "We've been here two days, and we've already been invited to church. Do we look that sinful?"

"It's a small town," Kirsten said, climbing into the passenger seat. "Everyone goes to church. It's probably the law."

Emmaline chuckled as she started the car. "Let's just focus on getting through today."

The road back to the house was lined with towering oaks and sprawling fields, their golden hues glowing in the late afternoon light. As they turned into the long, winding driveway, the mansion loomed ahead, its weathered facade looking a little less menacing in the soft glow of sunset.

"It's starting to feel like home," Emmaline murmured, though a small part of her wondered what secrets the house—and the town—were keeping.

CHAPTER 4

The late afternoon sun filtered through the canopy of ancient oaks surrounding the property, casting long shadows over the yard where Joe and his nephews were still hard at work. The hum of hedge trimmers and the steady thunk of shovels filled the air, blending with the rustle of leaves in the slight breeze.

Inside, the witches had made noticeable progress. The living room was no longer a complete disaster. The floor had been swept, most of the furniture dusted, and they'd even managed to unearth an old bookshelf tucked into a corner. Though the house was still far from perfect, there was a growing sense that it was slowly beginning to feel lived in again.

Kirsten stood by one of the windows, watching the groundskeeper's crew through the wavy glass panes. "They're surprisingly good at this," she remarked, sipping from a bottle of water. "I was expecting more slacking."

"Probably because Joe looks like he could kill a man with a rusty spade," Moira quipped from the couch, where she was sprawled out, clearly done with cleaning for the day.

Emmaline walked in, carrying a tray of glasses and a pitcher of lemonade. "Be nice. They're helping us out."

"I *am* being nice," Moira said, sitting up just enough to grab a glass. "I'm complimenting their fear-based work ethic."

Kirsten shook her head and turned back to the window. "Jeremy looks like he's ready to pass out."

"I'm not sure if that's from the heat or from sheer laziness," Emmaline said as she poured herself a glass. "Either way, they're earning that lemonade."

Moira stretched lazily. "Should we bring it out to them? You know, as a show of goodwill—or is that too neighborly?"

Kirsten grabbed the tray before Moira could object. "I'll do it. Last thing we need is you trying to socialize."

Moira grinned, but said nothing as Kirsten made her way outside.

The afternoon sun hit Kirsten hard as she stepped onto the front porch, the heat pressing down on her shoulders like a heavy blanket. She squinted against the glare and made her way toward the group, tray balanced carefully in her hands.

Joe Wilkes was trimming back a particularly unruly patch of overgrown bushes, his movements precise and practiced. Clay was working nearby, digging a trench around one of the flower beds, while Jeremy leaned on his shovel, looking half-asleep.

"Break time," Kirsten called, setting the tray down on a nearby stump.

Joe straightened, wiping his brow with a worn handkerchief. "Appreciate it," he said, his voice as gruff as ever. He grabbed a glass and took a long sip before nodding his thanks.

Clay followed suit, offering her a polite smile as he reached for a glass. "Thanks, ma'am. It's hotter than the devil's armpit out here."

Kirsten chuckled. "Welcome to Louisiana."

Jeremy, meanwhile, took his time sauntering over, his expression one of exaggerated suffering. He grabbed a glass, drained half of it in one gulp, and let out a dramatic sigh. "You know, manual labor really isn't my thing."

Joe shot him a look. "Quit whining and drink your lemonade."

Jeremy rolled his eyes but didn't argue.

Kirsten leaned against a nearby tree, watching them for a moment. "You guys from around here?"

"Born and raised," Clay said, wiping the back of his neck. "Joe's been working these parts since before I was born. Figured we'd help him out for a few bucks."

"Big family?" Kirsten asked, more out of curiosity than anything else.

Clay nodded. "Big enough. Most folks around here are related one way or another."

"Yeah, we noticed," Kirsten said, smiling. "Small town life, right?"

Jeremy snorted. "Small town life is boring. Nothing ever happens here."

Joe's expression darkened slightly, but he said nothing, focusing instead on finishing his lemonade. Kirsten caught the shift in his demeanor but decided not to press.

"Well, thanks again for helping out," she said after a beat. "We'll be here a while, so I'm sure we'll see plenty of each other."

Joe gave her a curt nod. "Y'all let us know if you need anything else."

With that, they went back to work, and Kirsten headed back inside, the unease lingering in the back of her mind. Something about Joe's reaction had struck her as odd, but she couldn't quite put her finger on it.

Later that evening, the three witches gathered in the kitchen, sorting through their groceries. The sun had dipped below the horizon, and the house was bathed in the soft glow of the old lamps they'd managed to get working.

"Did anyone else notice how weird Joe got when Jeremy mentioned nothing happens here?" Kirsten asked, stacking cans of soup in the cupboard.

Emmaline paused, frowning slightly. "I did. He loo ked... uncomfortable."

"Maybe it's just small-town stuff," Moira said, unpacking a loaf of bread. "You know how people get. They don't like outsiders poking around."

"Maybe," Kirsten said, though she didn't sound convinced.

Emmaline set down the box she was holding and leaned against the counter. "It's something to keep in mind. We're new here. People are going to watch us closely, especially since we moved into *that* house."

Moira smirked. "You mean the spooky mansion that looks like it came straight out of a gothic novel? Yeah, that might raise a few eyebrows."

"Exactly," Emmaline said. "Let's keep a low profile for now. The last thing we need is to stir up trouble."

"Agreed," Kirsten said. "But low profile or not, we're going to have to meet more of the locals eventually."

Emmaline sighed, rubbing her temples. "I know. And apparently, that starts with Sunday mass."

Moira groaned loudly. "We're not actually going, are we?"

Kirsten shrugged. "Why not? It's a good way to meet people, and it'll make us look normal."

"We are *not* normal," Moira said, pointing at her. "We're three witches living in a creepy old house on the edge of town. We're the exact opposite of normal."

"Which is why we need to *pretend* to be normal," Emmaline said, giving her a pointed look. "At least until we figure out what's what."

Moira muttered something under her breath but didn't argue further.

As the night deepened, the house settled into an eerie quiet, the only sounds the creak of the floorboards and the occasional rustle of the wind outside. Emmaline sat by the window, staring out into the darkness. The woods beyond the yard were a wall of black, impenetrable and still.

"We'll figure it out," she murmured to herself, though she wasn't entirely sure what *it* was. The house, the town, the unease that had crept into her bones since they arrived—whatever it was, they'd figure it out.

They had to. From the shadows of the tree line, someone watched.

Still. Silent. Barely breathing.

The flickering glow of candlelight inside the house threw distorted reflections against the window. And then, for the briefest moment, the girl at the window looked up.

Her eyes locked onto the darkness.

Onto *him.*

He didn't move.

Didn't blink.

He held his breath, muscles coiled tight, waiting.

The girl's gaze searched the woods, her face illuminated by the warm, golden light behind her. For a heartbeat, it felt as if she *knew.* As if she could *see* through the thick veil of shadows.

And then she *turned away from the window*

His pulse quickened.

Time to go.

A slow, measured step back. Then another. And another.

The trees swallowed him whole, the dense blackness wrapping around him like a second skin. He moved like a shadow slipping between the branches, vanishing without a trace.

From inside the house, Emmaline turned to get into her bed, unaware that someone had been watching her from tree line.

CHAPTER 5

Sunday morning came far too quickly for the witches. The sun shone brightly through the warped windowpanes, casting streaks of light across the half-cleaned living room. Outside, the grounds were quiet, the work Joe and his nephews had done making a noticeable difference in the once-overgrown yard.

"I can't believe we're doing this," Moira grumbled as she stood in front of a tall mirror, tugging on a light jacket. "Church? Really? I thought the whole point of moving here was to avoid nosy small-town people."

"The point was to inherit a house and maybe not die in it," Kirsten said, pulling her hair into a ponytail. "Besides, it's just one service. We'll make an appearance, meet a few people, and leave."

Moira muttered something inaudible as she adjusted her jacket. "Fine. But if someone starts talking about 'saving' us, I'm out."

Emmaline emerged from the hallway, dressed simply in jeans and a white blouse. She looked calm, though the tension in her shoulders suggested otherwise. "Let's just be polite and get through it. This is a good chance to learn more about the town."

Moira raised an eyebrow. "Learn what, exactly? Who's most likely to form a mob if they find out we're witches?"

"Maybe," Emmaline said with a smirk. "Or maybe just figure out how normal people around here behave."

"Normal people," Moira repeated, grabbing her purse. "We'll blend right in."

St. Mark's Church was a small, modest building with white clapboard siding and a tall steeple that looked slightly askew, as though it had been pushed by a strong wind years ago and never quite recovered. The parking lot was already half-full when they arrived, mostly with pickup trucks and older sedans.

The moment they stepped out of the car, they could feel the weight of curious eyes on them. Small clusters of townsfolk stood by the entrance, chatting quietly, their conversations pausing as the newcomers approached.

"Here we go," Kirsten muttered under her breath, offering a tight smile to an older couple who gave them a once-over.

As they reached the entrance, a cheerful voice called out to them. "Mornin', ladies!"

They turned to see Mabel, the stout cashier from Patterson's Groceries, making her way toward them. She was dressed in a simple floral dress and carried a well-worn leather-bound Bible in one hand.

"Didn't think y'all would make it," Mabel said, smiling broadly. "It's good to see new faces in town. Makes things more lively."

"Good morning," Emmaline said politely. "Thanks for the invitation."

Mabel waved a hand. "Oh, it's nothing. Folks around here like to keep things friendly." She leaned in slightly, lowering her voice. "Don't mind the staring. People are just curious. We don't get many newcomers, especially not in the old Pritchard house."

Moira's eyes flicked toward a group of women near the door, who were whispering among themselves while casting furtive glances their way. "Curious, huh? Feels more like we're on trial."

Mabel chuckled. "Small towns, dear. Everyone knows everyone's business, and when there's new business to know, people get nosy. You'll get used to it."

"Can't wait," Moira muttered.

"Well, come on inside," Mabel said, gesturing toward the door. "Pastor Williams is a good man. He'll make you feel welcome."

With little choice but to follow, the witches stepped into the church, the scent of old wood and faintly musty hymnals washing over them.

The moment they crossed the threshold, Moira leaned in close to Emmaline and Kirsten, whispering with mock shock, "I didn't burst into flames!"

Emmaline snorted softly, biting back a laugh, while Kirsten rolled her eyes and gave Moira a playful nudge. The three of them exchanged amused glances before taking seats near the back, doing their best to remain inconspicuous.

The service began with a hymn that most of the congregation seemed to know by heart, their voices rising in unison. The witches remained politely silent, occasionally glancing at one another with the faintest hint of amusement.

When the hymn ended, Pastor Williams, a tall man with salt-and-pepper hair and a deep, calming voice, stepped up to the pulpit. He welcomed everyone warmly, his eyes briefly lingering on the newcomers before launching into his sermon.

"Today's message is about faith," he began, his voice echoing slightly in the small space. "Faith in ourselves, faith in our community, and most importantly, faith in the Lord to guide us through times of uncertainty."

Moira leaned toward Kirsten, whispering, "Does faith include faith that this chair won't break under me?"

"Shh," Emmaline hissed, though her lips twitched in amusement.

Pastor Williams continued, oblivious to their quiet commentary. "In a world full of doubt, it can be hard to trust. Hard to believe in things we can't always see. But that's what faith is. Believing without seeing. Trusting that we are being watched over, even when we feel alone."

"Sounds a lot like our magic," Kirsten whispered. "Except with fewer candles."

Emmaline gave her a sideways glance. "If he starts talking about summoning circles, I'm out of here."

Moira covered her mouth to stifle a laugh.

"Faith is also about community," Pastor Williams went on, his tone growing more earnest. "About coming together, supporting one another, and keeping the bonds that hold us strong."

At that, Moira leaned over again, whispering, "Think they'd still want to bond with us if they knew about the pentagram in our attic?"

Kirsten barely managed to keep her composure, while Emmaline shot her a warning look. "Keep it together," she whispered back, though even she couldn't hide her amusement.

The sermon wrapped up with another hymn, and by the time Pastor Williams gave the final blessing, the witches were more than ready to make their exit.

People lingered, chatting in small groups. The witches debated making a quiet exit, but Mabel intercepted them before they could slip out.

"Y'all doing anything after this?" she asked brightly.

"We were planning on heading back to the house," Emmaline said. "Still a lot of cleaning to do."

"Well, if you're not too busy, you should stop by the diner for lunch. A bunch of us usually head over after service. It's a good way to get to know folks."

Emmaline hesitated, glancing at Kirsten and Moira. Kirsten gave a small shrug, while Moira looked like she wanted to melt into the floor.

"That sounds nice," Emmaline said after a moment. "We'll stop by."

The diner, a squat building with a weathered sign that read *Ruby's*, was bustling when they arrived. The smell of frying bacon and fresh coffee wafted through the air as they stepped inside, and the chatter of conversation filled the room.

Mabel waved them over to a large booth near the window, where several other townsfolk were already seated. Among them was Joe Wilkes, who nodded stiffly in greeting, and Clay, who offered them a friendly smile.

"Glad y'all could make it," Mabel said, sliding into the booth. "This here's Ruby, the owner. Best cook in town."

Ruby, a stout woman in her sixties with sharp eyes and a no-nonsense demeanor, gave them a once-over before nodding in approval. "Welcome. Hope you're hungry."

They ordered simple meals—burgers, fries, and iced tea—and tried to ignore the subtle glances from other tables. Conversation flowed easily enough, mostly small talk about the weather and the work being done on the Pritchard house.

At one point, Clay leaned over and asked, "So, what brings y'all to Albany? Not many folks move here."

"We inherited the house," Emmaline said. "Didn't really plan on it, but here we are."

"Big place," Clay said. "Must be a lot of work."

"It is," Kirsten said with a sigh. "But we're making progress."

Joe, who had been silent for most of the meal, finally spoke. "Pritchard place has a long history. You be careful out there."

Emmaline met his gaze, sensing there was more behind his words than simple concern. "We will."

Mabel, sensing the shift in tone, leaned forward. "Old houses like that tend to have stories, you know? Some folks say it's just bad luck. Others... well, they get ideas."

"Bad luck?" Moira asked, her interest piqued. "Like what?"

Joe shrugged, but his eyes were serious. "Accidents. Strange things happening. Couple of folks swore it was cursed. Most people just stay away."

"Superstitions," Mabel added quickly, trying to keep the conversation light. "Nothing to worry about. Just small-town gossip."

"Right," Emmaline said, though she could feel the unease settling in her chest. "Small-town gossip."

By the time they left the diner, the sun was high in the sky, and the heat was almost stifling. The ride back to the mansion was quiet, each of them lost in thought.

"That was... interesting," Moira said as they pulled into the driveway.

"Could've been worse," Kirsten replied. "At least no one brought out pitchforks."

"Yet," Moira added darkly.

Emmaline parked the car and turned off the engine. "We made a good impression. That's what matters."

"For now," Kirsten said, stepping out of the car. "But we'll have to be careful. People are watching us."

Emmaline glanced toward the house, its shadow stretching long across the yard. "Let them watch."

CHAPTER 6

Monday morning arrived quietly, the stillness of the woods broken only by the occasional call of a bird or the distant hum of a truck passing along the road. The house, now slightly less cluttered after days of cleaning, still had an air of abandonment about it. Despite their best efforts, there was a lingering scent of old wood, dust, and something faintly floral.

Emmaline stood in the kitchen, pouring herself a cup of coffee and watching the sunlight filter through the trees outside. It was peaceful, almost deceptively so, considering the unease that had taken root in the back of her mind after the conversation at the diner.

"Still thinking about what Joe said?" Kirsten asked, walking into the kitchen and grabbing a mug.

Emmaline didn't answer immediately. She took a sip of her coffee, her gaze still fixed on the woods. "You think he was serious?"

Kirsten shrugged, pouring her coffee. "He seemed serious. But it could just be one of those things small towns do—make up ghost stories and curses to keep life interesting."

"Maybe." Emmaline set her cup down, leaning against the counter. "But something about the way he said it felt… different. Like he wasn't just telling us a story."

Before Kirsten could respond, Moira entered, yawning dramatically and stretching her arms over her head. "Morning, witches. What's on the agenda today? More cleaning? More creeping out the locals?"

"We were just talking about Joe," Kirsten said, raising an eyebrow. "You know, the ominous 'be careful out there' speech?"

"Oh, that." Moira waved a hand dismissively. "I wouldn't lose sleep over it. Every old house has its weird stories. Besides, if there is something creepy going on, we're witches. We're practically built for dealing with creepy."

"Sure, but I'd rather not find out what kind of creepy he meant," Emmaline said, grabbing her cup again.

"Speaking of creepy," Kirsten said, changing the subject, "I was thinking we should check out the attic. We've barely scratched the surface of this place, and if there's anything interesting—or cursed—it's probably up there."

Moira's eyes lit up. "Ooh, an attic adventure? Count me in."

"I'm not sure 'adventure' is the word I'd use," Emmaline muttered, though she couldn't deny her curiosity. "But you're right. We should see what's up there."

The entrance to the attic was a small, square door at the end of upstairs hallway. Moira was nominated to open the creaky old door, which groaned in protest as its door slowly swung open to reveal an old staircase.

"This staircase looks like it could collapse at any second," Kirsten said, eyeing it warily.

"Only one way to find out," Moira said with a grin, stepping onto the first step.

Emmaline and Kirsten exchanged a glance before following her up, the stairs creaking ominously with each step.

The attic was dimly lit, the only source of light a small, dusty window at the far end. Cobwebs hung thick in the corners, and the air was stale, carrying a faint metallic scent. Old trunks, crates, and furniture covered in white sheets filled the space, casting strange shadows in the dim light.

"Well, this is sufficiently creepy," Moira said, stepping carefully over a pile of discarded picture frames. "I give it a solid eight out of ten on the haunted scale."

"Let's just take a quick look around," Emmaline said, her eyes scanning the room. "See if there's anything useful—or weird."

They moved carefully through the space, pulling back sheets and opening trunks. Most of what they found was mundane—old clothes, faded photographs, and stacks of yellowed newspapers. But as they reached the far end of the attic, Kirsten paused, her eyes narrowing at something half-buried beneath a pile of broken chairs.

"What's that?" she asked, pointing.

Emmaline and Moira joined her, and together they uncovered what appeared to be an old, hand-carved chest. The wood was dark and intricately etched with symbols none of them recognized.

Moira ran a finger over one of the carvings, frowning. "This looks... weird."

"Understatement of the year," Kirsten said, crouching down to get a closer look. "You think it's locked?"

Emmaline knelt beside her, examining the chest. "If it is, the lock's hidden. I don't see anything obvious."

"Well, there's only one way to find out," Moira said, reaching for the lid.

"Wait!" Emmaline said quickly, grabbing her wrist. "We don't know what's in there. It could be cursed."

Moira gave her a look. "Come on. It's probably just full of old junk."

"Maybe," Emmaline said cautiously. "But let's not take any chances. We'll bring it downstairs and figure out how to open it safely."

Moira sighed but didn't argue, stepping back as Emmaline and Kirsten carefully lifted the chest.

By the time they got the chest downstairs, they were all more than ready for a break. They set it down in the living room, the weight of the discovery hanging heavy in the air.

"So," Kirsten said, flopping onto the couch. "What's the plan? We break out the big spellbook and see if we can figure out what this thing is?"

"Something like that," Emmaline said, still eyeing the chest warily. "But first, we need to do a little more research. Maybe ask around town."

"Oh, great," Moira said, rolling her eyes. "More mingling with the locals. Can't wait."

Emmaline ignored her, already lost in thought. Whatever was in that chest, she had a feeling it was connected to the strange vibe of the house—and possibly the warnings they'd received.

She just hoped they weren't about to open a door they couldn't close.

After cleaning up and grabbing a quick lunch, the witches decided to head into town again. The streets were quiet, most of the shops closed for the afternoon.

They made their way to Patterson's Groceries, figuring it was as good a place as any to start asking questions.

Mabel greeted them with a smile as they entered. "Back already?"

"We needed a few more things," Emmaline said, grabbing a basket. "And, well, we were wondering..."

Mabel raised an eyebrow. "Wondering what?"

Emmaline hesitated for a moment before asking, "Do you know anything about the Pritchard family? The ones who lived in our house before us?"

Mabel's smile faltered slightly, and she glanced around as if making sure no one else was listening. "Not much, really. Just what everyone around here knows. The family kept to themselves. Had some strange habits, folks said."

"Strange how?" Kirsten asked, leaning on the counter.

Mabel lowered her voice. "Just... odd things. People said they heard noises coming from the house at night. Saw lights in the windows when no one was supposed to be home. That kind of thing."

"Great," Moira muttered. "So it really *is* haunted."

Mabel gave them a pointed look. "Whatever it was, no one's lived there for a long time. People around here don't like to talk about it much."

Emmaline nodded slowly, filing the information away. "Thanks, Mabel. We appreciate it."

"Y'all be careful out there," Mabel said, her tone serious. "That house has a way of getting under your skin."

Emmaline forced a smile. "We will."

As they left the store, the unease from earlier returned, stronger this time.

"Okay," Kirsten said as they climbed into the car. "So, what's the verdict? Haunted, cursed, or just plain weird?"

"Maybe all of the above," Emmaline said quietly. "But whatever's going on, we need to figure it out. Fast."

Moira sighed, slumping in her seat. "This just keeps getting better."

Emmaline started the car, the engine rumbling to life. As they drove back toward the mansion, the road ahead seemed longer and darker than before.

And somewhere in the back of her mind, Emmaline couldn't shake the feeling that they were being watched.

CHAPTER 7

By the time they returned to the house, the oppressive heat of the day had waned, leaving behind a warm breeze that rustled through the ancient oaks lining the driveway. The mansion's weathered facade gleamed faintly in the late afternoon light, giving it an almost serene appearance. Inside, however, serenity was nowhere to be found.

Moira, still riding high from the absurdity of the morning, decided it was the perfect time to focus on a deeply personal project: decorating her bedroom.

"I need to make this place feel more... me," she declared, her voice echoing through the upstairs hallway as she lugged a large cardboard box into her room.

From the living room below, Emmaline glanced up toward the ceiling, which creaked ominously under

Moira's movements. "What do you mean by 'more you'? And do we even want to know?"

"You'll see," Moira called down cheerfully, disappearing into her room with the door left slightly ajar.

Kirsten, perched on the arm of the couch with a half-empty cup of coffee in hand, gave Emmaline a wary look. "Should we be worried?"

"Always," Emmaline replied with a sigh, flipping through an old leather-bound book they had found in the attic earlier. "But it's Moira, so worrying is pretty much a full-time job."

For the next twenty minutes, faint thuds and the sound of shifting furniture drifted down from Moira's room. Occasionally, there was a muffled exclamation, followed by something heavy being dropped.

"I'm fine!" Moira yelled at one point, though no one had asked.

Eventually, she reappeared, dramatically stepping into the living room with an air of triumphant mischief. In her arms, she cradled what appeared to be a polished wooden statue about a foot tall. At first glance, it looked like a vaguely abstract sculpture—until the details came into focus.

"Is that...?" Kirsten started, leaning forward with a frown.

"Yep," Moira said, grinning as she placed the statue squarely on the coffee table. "A penis. A very distinguished one, if I do say so myself."

Emmaline stared at it, blinking. "Why?"

"Why not?" Moira shot back, looking positively delighted by their reactions. "It's tasteful, it's bold, and it makes a statement."

Kirsten leaned closer, squinting at the statue's intricate carvings. "What statement? That you're starting a penis museum?"

"Exactly," Moira said without missing a beat. "I call this piece *Confidence*. You'll notice the flawless symmetry and the impressive girth."

Emmaline buried her face in her hands, trying—and failing—not to laugh. "You're impossible."

"Oh, but wait, there's more!" Moira's grin widened as she reached into the box she had carried downstairs and pulled out another, smaller statue, placing it next to the first one. "This one is called *Optimism*."

"You're ridiculous," Kirsten muttered, though she was clearly trying not to laugh.

Moira gave an exaggerated bow. "Thank you, thank you. But the pièce de résistance awaits." She set the box down on the floor and opened it with a dramatic creak, revealing a small wooden chest inside. With a flourish, she lifted the lid to reveal an array of brightly colored objects in various shapes and sizes.

Emmaline leaned forward, frowning. "Are those—?"

"Yep," Moira said, grinning wickedly. "Butt plugs. For amusement purposes only."

Kirsten burst out laughing, nearly spilling her coffee. "Why do you even have these?"

"Because life is too short not to own a box of novelty butt plugs," Moira said, holding up a bright pink one shaped like a unicorn tail. The synthetic tail swayed slightly in the air as she twirled it around. "Look at this! It's whimsical."

Emmaline reached for a nearby throw pillow and lobbed it at Moira's head. "You're insane."

Moira ducked, narrowly avoiding the pillow. "Insane? No, no. I'm a visionary. One day, people will thank me for bringing humor and class to an otherwise dull world."

Kirsten wiped a tear from her eye, still laughing. "You know, if this is your way of blending in with small-town life, we're doomed."

Moira placed the wooden chest on a shelf with a satisfied smile. "You laugh now, but when this place becomes a tourist hotspot for eccentric decor, don't say I didn't warn you."

Later that evening, after they'd recovered from Moira's antics, the witches gathered in the kitchen for something slightly more serious: attempting a simple protection spell. The earlier conversation with Mabel, coupled with the strange history of the house, had left them feeling unsettled, and they figured a little extra magical insurance couldn't hurt.

"Okay," Emmaline said, setting a small bowl of dried herbs on the counter. "This spell is supposed to create a protective barrier around the house. It's simple—light the herbs, say the incantation, and let the smoke do its thing."

Kirsten peered into the bowl. "What's in there?"

"Lavender, sage, rosemary... the usual stuff," Emmaline replied, lighting a match. "Nothing fancy."

Moira leaned against the counter, munching on a bag of chips. "So we're basically turning the house into a giant incense stick. Got it."

"Do you want protection from bad luck or not?" Emmaline asked, arching an eyebrow.

Moira shrugged. "Fine. Do your thing, witch queen."

Emmaline rolled her eyes but smiled as she lit the herbs. A thin tendril of smoke curled upward, filling the air with a calming, earthy scent. She began to recite the incantation, her voice low and steady, the words flowing easily from her lips.

At first, everything seemed to be going perfectly. The smoke drifted lazily around the room, creating a soft, shimmering haze. But just as Emmaline finished the final word of the spell, a sudden gust of wind rushed through the kitchen, snuffing out the flame and scattering the herbs across the counter.

"Uh... was that supposed to happen?" Kirsten asked, taking a cautious step back.

"No," Emmaline said, eyes wide. "Definitely not."

Before any of them could react, the smoke thickened, swirling rapidly into a small, dense cloud near the ceiling. For a brief moment, it hovered there, pulsing with an almost mischievous energy.

Moira pointed upward. "I don't like that. This can't be good."

The cloud quivered once more before bursting like a confetti cannon, showering the entire room—and its occupants—in a fine, glittery dust.

Kirsten coughed, waving her hands in front of her face. "What the hell just happened?"

"I have no idea," Emmaline said, brushing glitter out of her hair. "That wasn't part of the spell."

Moira, now thoroughly coated in glitter, held up her hands, which sparkled under the dim kitchen lights. "Did we just accidentally summon a glitter bomb?"

"Looks like it," Kirsten muttered, examining her glitter-covered arms. "Great. Now we're cursed *and* fabulous."

Moira grabbed a handful of glitter from the counter and let it fall through her fingers. "Honestly? I'm not mad about it. If this is what bad luck looks like, it's kind of festive."

Emmaline groaned, rubbing her temples. "We need to clean this up before it spreads."

"Too late," Kirsten said, pointing at the floor, which was already sparkling like a disco ball.

As they began the arduous process of cleaning up, Moira couldn't resist making one final comment.

"Well," she said, grinning, "at least if anyone accuses us of being witches, we can tell them we're more about sparkles and penis statues than dark magic."

Emmaline laughed despite herself. "Yeah, that's definitely going on the brochure."

CHAPTER 8

The scent of grilled meat hung thick in the air, mingling with the rich, earthy aroma of freshly cut grass and the faint tang of wood smoke. The town barbecue was in full swing, held in the large open field behind St. Mark's Church. Long picnic tables stretched across the grass, covered in red-and-white checkered tablecloths. Families gathered in clusters, chatting over plates piled high with ribs, brisket, and baked beans, while children ran barefoot across the field, their laughter ringing out over the steady hum of conversation.

Nearby, a group of older men stood around a grill, tending to the food with the air of seasoned pitmasters. Smoke billowed from the stacked pits, and the sizzling sound of fat dripping onto hot coals provided a steady backdrop to the lively chatter.

The witches stood near the edge of the gathering, taking in the scene. Emmaline squinted against the afternoon sun, already regretting her choice of jeans in the stifling Louisiana heat. Kirsten, ever practical, had opted for loose linen pants and a tank top, while Moira, true to form, wore a flowing black sundress that somehow made her look both out of place and perfectly at home.

"This is... quaint," Moira said, her tone laced with mild disdain. "Do they hold barbecues every time someone new moves into town?"

"No," Kirsten said, smirking. "This is just their way of keeping an eye on us without being obvious about it."

Emmaline sighed. "Let's just be friendly, blend in, and try not to make it weird."

"Define 'weird,'" Moira muttered as a small child ran past, nearly colliding with her. She gave the kid an exaggerated glare before turning back to her friends. "Because I'm pretty sure showing up to a barbecue dressed like a funeral director already earned us that label."

Before Emmaline could respond, a familiar voice called out from across the field. "Afternoon, ladies!"

They turned to see Mabel approaching, balancing a large plate of ribs in one hand and a plastic cup of sweet tea in the other. She was dressed in a brightly colored blouse and capri pants, looking every bit the part of a small-town hostess. Her sunhat bobbed slightly as she walked, its wide brim shielding her from the afternoon glare.

"Glad y'all could make it," Mabel said, her smile broad. "I was worried you might skip out."

"We wouldn't miss it," Emmaline said politely, though she suspected that skipping out would have only fueled more gossip.

"Good, good," Mabel said, nodding in approval. "Come on, let me introduce you to a few folks."

They followed Mabel across the field, weaving through groups of townsfolk who all paused mid-conversation to glance at the newcomers. Some offered polite nods, while others whispered behind their hands.

At one of the picnic tables, Joe Wilkes sat with his nephews, Clay and Jeremy, their plates piled high with food. Joe, as usual, looked as though he'd rather be anywhere else, while Clay greeted them with a friendly wave.

"Hey there," Clay said, grinning as they approached. "Y'all enjoying the barbecue?"

"It's... something," Moira said, eyeing the mountain of ribs on his plate. "You planning to eat all of that yourself?"

"Gotta fuel up for more yard work," Clay said with a wink. "Y'all have a lot of bushes."

"Don't remind me," Emmaline muttered, though her lips twitched in amusement.

Jeremy, who had been picking at a plate of coleslaw, gave them a halfhearted nod before turning his attention back to his food. He looked about as enthusiastic as Joe, though in Jeremy's case, it seemed more like boredom than disdain.

Joe wiped his hands on a napkin and leaned back in his chair, giving the witches a critical once-over. "Y'all settling in alright?"

"More or less," Emmaline said. "Still a lot of work to do."

Joe grunted in response, though whether it was approval or something else entirely was unclear.

"So," Clay said, leaning back slightly, "how's the house treating y'all? Must be a big change, moving into a place like that."

"It's definitely… different," Kirsten said, choosing her words carefully. "But we're making it work."

Moira caught Clay's eye and raised an eyebrow. "You sound like you've been there before."

"Only once," Clay admitted. "When I was a kid. My uncle did some work on the roof back then. I remember thinking it looked like something out of one of those old horror movies."

Moira smirked. "You're not wrong."

Clay chuckled, the sound low and pleasant. "Well, if you need help with anything—besides the yard—I'm around."

"Thanks," Moira said, her voice unusually soft. She wasn't used to people offering help without expecting something in return, and the sincerity in Clay's tone caught her off guard.

Kirsten, noticing the subtle shift in Moira's demeanor, gave Emmaline a quick nudge, as if to say, *Are you seeing this?*

As they continued chatting, a new voice cut through the hum of conversation—a voice that practically oozed with smug self-assurance.

"Well, well, if it isn't our mysterious new residents."

The witches turned to see a man approaching, his gait lazy yet purposeful. He was in his mid-thirties, with slicked-back hair, a tan that looked just a little too perfect, and a grin that was far too confident. He wore a button-down shirt with the top three buttons undone, exposing a gold chain resting on his chest.

"Ladies," he said, flashing a smile that might have been charming if it weren't so obviously practiced. "Name's Kevin. Kevin Rawlins."

Moira exchanged a glance with Kirsten, who looked like she was already bracing for whatever nonsense was about to come out of his mouth.

Kevin extended a hand to Emmaline, who hesitated for a split second before shaking it. His grip was firm—too firm, as if he were trying to prove something.

"Welcome to Albany," Kevin said, his grin widening. "You ever need anything—a car, a tour of the town, a dinner companion—you just let ol' Kevin know."

"Thanks," Emmaline said, her tone polite but cool.

Kevin turned his attention to Moira, his eyes flicking over her in a way that made her skin crawl. "And who might you be?"

"Out of your league," Moira said flatly, crossing her arms.

Clay choked on his drink, while Kirsten bit back a laugh. Even Joe's expression shifted slightly, though whether it was amusement or annoyance, it was hard to tell.

Kevin, to his credit, recovered quickly. "Feisty. I like that."

"Good for you," Moira said, turning away pointedly.

Emmaline cleared her throat, eager to change the subject. "So, Kevin, what do you do around here?"

"Sell cars," Kevin said, leaning against the edge of the table. "Best used car dealer in the parish. Might even say I'm God's gift to transportation."

"And modest too," Kirsten muttered under her breath.

Kevin ignored her, his attention still focused on Moira, who was now very deliberately not looking at him. "You know," he said, "if you ever get tired of... whatever it is you do, you could come work for me. Pretty face like yours could sell a lot of cars."

Before Moira could unleash whatever scathing re-mark was brewing, Mabel stepped in. "Alright, Kevin, why don't you go bother someone else for a while?"

Kevin held up his hands in mock surrender. "Alright, alright. No harm meant." He gave Moira one last grin before sauntering off, his gold chain catching the sun-light.

"That guy's a walking cliché," Kirsten said once he was out of earshot.

"More like a walking HR violation," Moira muttered.

"Don't mind Kevin," Mabel said with a sigh. "He means well, but... well, he's Kevin."

"That explains a lot," Emmaline said, shaking her head.

As the sun dipped lower in the sky, the barbecue began to wind down. Children chased fireflies across the field, their laughter mingling with the soft hum of crickets. The warm glow of string lights draped around the picnic area bathed everything in a golden hue, casting long shadows over the grass.

The witches lingered for a while longer, enjoying the rare moment of peace. Clay found his way back over to them, this time striking up a quieter conversation with Moira. They stood off to the side, the flickering light catching the amused tilt of Moira's lips as Clay told her some story that made her laugh—a genuine, soft sound that Emmaline couldn't remember hearing in a while.

"Looks like someone's making friends," Kirsten murmured, nudging Emmaline.

"Let's hope he's not as much trouble as Kevin," Emmaline said with a smirk.

As they finally made their way back to the car, Moira lagged behind for a moment, exchanging a few last words with Clay before catching up.

"You two looked cozy," Kirsten teased as they climbed into the car.

"Shut up," Moira said, though her tone lacked its usual bite. "He's... nice."

Emmaline started the car, the engine rumbling to life. "Nice is good. We could use a little nice."

As they drove back toward the mansion, the conversation shifted toward their plans for the upcoming full moon ritual. They still had preparations to make, and after the events of the past few days, none of them wanted to take any chances.

Whatever was coming, they would be ready.

Or at least, they hoped they would be.

CHAPTER 9

The morning sun rose over Albany, casting long shadows through the ancient oaks that loomed over the property. The mansion, though still a work in progress, looked a bit less abandoned after days of cleaning and clearing. The witches had done their best to make it livable—though the peeling paint and sagging shutters still gave it the air of something straight out of a Southern Gothic tale.

Emmaline sipped her coffee from the front porch, her green eyes scanning the quiet road in front of the house. Despite the early hour, she couldn't shake the feeling that someone was watching. The locals had been polite enough at the barbecue, but she knew small-town hospitality came with strings attached—and curious eyes.

"They're probably peeking through their curtains, wondering what we're up to," Moira said, stepping onto the porch with her own cup of coffee. Dressed in a loose black tank top and leggings, she looked more like someone ready for yoga than a witch preparing for another day of yard work.

"They'll get bored eventually," Emmaline replied, though she wasn't entirely convinced.

"Doubtful," Kirsten said, joining them. She wore jeans and a plain gray T-shirt, her blonde hair tied back in a ponytail. "Small towns thrive on gossip. We're the best thing to happen here since that McDonald's opened."

Emmaline snorted. "Great. Just what we need."

"Morning, ladies!" a familiar voice called from the driveway. They turned to see Joe Wilkes approaching, flanked by his nephews, Clay and Jeremy, both carrying shovels and rakes. Joe looked as grumpy as ever, while Clay flashed them an easy grin.

"Ready for more yard work?" Joe asked, not bothering to hide his lack of enthusiasm.

"We're always ready for more bushes," Moira said dryly, earning a chuckle from Clay.

Jeremy, as usual, offered nothing more than a brief nod before heading toward the overgrown flower beds. Clay lingered a moment longer, his eyes meeting Moira's with a hint of amusement.

"You sure you're up for this?" he asked. "It's gonna be a hot one today."

Moira raised an eyebrow. "You think I'm afraid of a little sweat?"

"Not at all," Clay said, his grin widening. "Just making sure you don't faint on us. I'd hate to have to carry you back inside."

"Please," Moira said with a smirk. "If anyone's getting carried, it'll be you."

Emmaline exchanged a glance with Kirsten, who gave a barely perceptible nod. There was definitely something brewing between those two.

They worked in relative silence for the next hour, the only sounds being the rustle of leaves, the scrape of shovels against dirt, and the occasional buzz of insects. The morning air grew heavier as the sun climbed higher, casting dappled patterns of light and shadow across the yard.

Moira found herself working alongside Clay more often than not. Whether by chance or design, he always seemed to be nearby, offering help or striking up small conversations.

"So," Clay said, leaning on his rake during a brief break, "how are you liking Albany so far?"

"It's... quaint," Moira said, choosing her words carefully. "A little nosy, but not bad."

"Yeah, people here can be... curious," Clay admitted. "It's just how it is. They don't mean any harm, though."

"I'll take your word for it," Moira said, brushing a strand of hair from her face. "You've lived here your whole life?"

Clay nodded. "Born and raised. It's not the most exciting place, but it's home." He hesitated for a moment before adding, "And, you know, it's nice to have something new around here for a change."

Moira felt a flicker of warmth at his words, but before she could respond, the sound of a car engine drew their attention.

A sleek, slightly battered sports car rolled up the driveway, its tires kicking up dust. The driver's side door opened, and out stepped Kevin Rawlins, his ever-present gold chain glinting in the sunlight.

"Oh, great," Kirsten muttered. "Just what we needed."

Kevin sauntered over, his grin as smug as ever. "Morning, ladies. Thought I'd drop by and see how y'all are settling in."

"How thoughtful," Emmaline said, her tone flat.

Kevin didn't seem to notice her lack of enthusiasm. His eyes flicked toward Moira, and his grin widened. "Hey there. You look like you could use a break. How about a ride into town? I know a great little diner."

Moira crossed her arms, her expression unimpressed. "I'm good, thanks."

Clay stepped forward, positioning himself subtly between Kevin and Moira. "I think she's fine where she is."

Kevin's smile faltered for a brief moment before he recovered. "No harm in offering," he said, holding up his hands in mock surrender. "Just being neighborly."

"Sure," Moira said, her voice dripping with sarcasm. "We'll call you if we need a used car or unsolicited advice."

Kevin chuckled, though the sound lacked its usual confidence. "Alright, alright. No need to get feisty." He gave them one last look before turning back to his car. "Y'all take care now."

As the car disappeared down the driveway, Moira let out a breath she hadn't realized she was holding.

"That guy really is a walking cliché," Kirsten said, shaking her head.

"More like a walking headache," Moira said flatly.

Clay turned to her, a hint of concern in his eyes. "You okay?"

"I'm fine," Moira said, offering a small smile. "Thanks for stepping in, though."

"Anytime," Clay said, his tone earnest.

By late afternoon, the yard was looking significantly better. The overgrown bushes had been trimmed back, the flower beds cleared, and a sense of order was beginning to emerge from the chaos.

Joe clapped his hands together, signaling the end of the day's work. "That'll do for today. We'll be back tomorrow to finish up the front."

"Thanks, Joe," Emmaline said, wiping sweat from her brow. "We appreciate it."

Joe gave a curt nod before heading toward his truck, with Jeremy following silently behind. Clay lingered a moment longer, his gaze flicking toward Moira.

"See you tomorrow?" he asked.

Moira nodded. "Yeah. See you tomorrow."

As Clay turned to leave, Emmaline and Kirsten exchanged knowing glances. Once he was out of earshot, Kirsten couldn't resist teasing.

"Getting cozy with the locals, huh?"

Moira rolled her eyes. "Don't start."

"Hey, I'm just saying," Kirsten said with a grin. "It's nice to have friends. Or more-than-friends."

"He's just being friendly," Moira insisted, though a faint blush crept up her neck.

"Uh-huh," Emmaline said, smirking. "Sure he is."

Despite their teasing, Moira couldn't help but smile as she headed back into the house. Maybe Albany wasn't so bad after all.

Inside, the witches gathered around the kitchen table, the mood lighter than it had been in days. The looming full moon ritual was still on their minds, but for now, they allowed themselves a moment of calm.

"We're making progress," Emmaline said, raising her glass of iced tea. "To fewer bushes and fewer visits from Kevin."

"I'll drink to that," Moira said, clinking her glass against Emmaline's.

As laughter filled the room, the shadows outside lengthened, and the first hints of twilight settled over the mansion. For the first time since they'd arrived, things felt... normal.

At least, for now.

CHAPTER 10

Morning light crept over Albany, Louisiana, casting a hazy golden glow across the streets. The town, small and unassuming, seemed to wake up in stages—first the birds, then the creak of front doors, and finally the low rumble of engines as trucks and sedans rolled onto the narrow roads. The air was thick with the scent of dew-covered grass.

At Patterson's Groceries, the heart of Albany's small business district, Mabel wiped down the counter for the third time that morning. The store smelled of freshly ground coffee, warm bread, and a hint of pine cleaner. Its narrow aisles were lined with neatly stocked shelves of canned goods, fresh produce, and locally made preserves. The single ceiling fan spun lazily, doing little to break the growing heat. Despite its modest size, Patterson's Groceries was more than just a store—it was a hub for the town's gossip and social life.

"Morning, Mabel," Joe Wilkes said as he walked in, tipping his worn baseball cap. His gruff voice carried easily across the quiet store. "Got any more of that pecan coffee?"

Mabel looked up from the counter, her sharp eyes softening when they met Joe's familiar face. "Fresh pot just finished brewing. Help yourself, Joe. You know where it is."

Joe poured himself a cup from the coffee station near the window. He was a man of habit, always taking his coffee black with just a dash of sugar. Leaning against the counter, he cradled the steaming mug in both hands. He wasn't one for idle chatter, but the silence hanging in the air felt heavier than usual.

"Busy morning?" Joe asked after a moment, more to break the quiet than anything else.

"Same as any other," Mabel replied, setting aside her dishrag. "Though folks are still talking about those new people at the old Pritchard place."

Joe took a slow sip of his coffee, his brow furrowing slightly. "Can't say I'm surprised. That house always did stir up talk. And now with them moving in, well... you know how people get."

Before Mabel could respond, the bell above the door jingled, signaling another customer. Kevin Rawlins sauntered in, his gold chain gleaming obnoxiously under the store's fluorescent lights. He wore a crisp white button-down shirt, half-unbuttoned to reveal far more chest than anyone wanted to see, and dark slacks that looked more suited for a nightclub than a small-town grocery run.

"Morning, beautiful," Kevin said with a grin that was as slick as the oil he used to keep his hair perfectly in place.

"Morning, Kevin," Mabel said with a sigh, already bracing herself for whatever nonsense he was about to spew. "What can I do for you today?"

"Just grabbing a bite before heading to the lot," Kevin said, snatching a pre-packaged sandwich from the cooler. "Business has been slow. Maybe I ought to swing by that mansion, see if they need a new ride.

Never know when someone's in the market for a dependable used car."

Joe set his mug down with a dull thud. "Doubt they're looking for what you're selling, Kevin."

Kevin chuckled, unfazed. "Hey, a man's gotta hustle. Besides, it's not just about business. Folks around here have a right to know who's living among them."

Mabel gave Kevin a hard look, her voice calm but firm. "They're fixing up that house and minding their own business. Maybe you should do the same."

Kevin held up his hands in his usual mock surrender. "Alright, alright. Just trying to be neighborly." He paid for his sandwich and turned toward the door. "Y'all have a good one. Don't get too spooked by our new residents."

As the door closed behind him, Mabel let out a breath she hadn't realized she was holding. "That boy's been trouble since the day he could walk."

Joe gave a grunt of agreement. "Too much time on his hands, not enough sense. People like him stir things up, make trouble where there ain't any."

Meanwhile, over at Ruby's Diner, the morning crowd was beginning to thin out. The diner, a relic of the 1950s with red vinyl booths and chrome accents, gleamed under the soft morning light filtering through the large front windows. The scent of sizzling bacon and freshly brewed coffee filled the air, mingling with the faint metallic tang of the old jukebox in the corner.

Ruby herself, a stout woman in her sixties with sharp eyes and a no-nonsense demeanor, moved between the tables with practiced ease. Her apron was smeared with flour and grease, evidence of a busy morning.

At a booth near the window, Clay Wilkes sat across from his cousin Jeremy, both of them eating their breakfast of eggs and bacon. Clay, his sleeves rolled up to reveal tanned forearms, leaned back in his seat, looking more relaxed than he had in days.

"Y'all heading back to the Pritchard place today?" Ruby asked as she refilled their coffee cups.

"Yeah, still got a ways to go with the yard," Clay said. "Place is a jungle."

Ruby gave him a knowing smile. "Bet it's not all bad. Heard you've been chatting up one of those new ladies."

Jeremy smirked, but Clay shot him a warning glance before turning back to Ruby. "Just being neighborly. They're new, figured it wouldn't hurt to lend a hand."

Ruby chuckled. "Well, you watch yourself. Folks around here are curious, and curious folks can get nosy."

"Ain't that the truth," Jeremy muttered, spearing a piece of bacon with his fork.

Clay gave a noncommittal shrug. "People talk. Doesn't mean we have to listen."

"True enough," Ruby said, turning back toward the counter. "But don't be surprised if they keep talking."

Across town, in a modest home shaded by an ancient oak tree, Pastor Williams sat at his kitchen table, reading over notes for his Sunday sermon. The scent of fresh biscuits and scrambled eggs filled the air as his wife, Ellen, set a plate in front of him.

"You think those newcomers will come to church again this Sunday?" Ellen asked, sitting down with her own plate.

Pastor Williams set down his pen, thoughtful. "Hard to say. But if they do, we'll welcome them like anyone else. It's what we're supposed to do."

"Some folks might not see it that way," Ellen said quietly.

"Then it'll be our job to remind them," Pastor Williams said, offering her a reassuring smile. "Everyone deserves a chance to be part of the community."

As they ate, the town outside stirred to life, its streets filling with the quiet buzz of everyday routines. Beneath the surface, however, a quiet tension lingered—an undercurrent of curiosity, fear, and something else, something unspoken. The newcomers had stirred the pot by moving into the old Pritchard house, and now everyone was waiting to see what might bubble to the surface.

CHAPTER 11

By late morning, the mansion felt slightly less like an abandoned relic and more like a home—or at least, the chaotic beginnings of one. Sunlight filtered through the cracked and slightly grimy windows, illuminating the dust motes that floated lazily in the air. The scent of lavender and sage hung faintly throughout the house, remnants of Kirsten's earlier efforts to ward off bad vibes with an overly enthusiastic smudging session—an effort that resulted in more coughing fits than spiritual cleansing.

"We're getting there," Emmaline said, standing in the middle of the living room with her hands on her hips like some kind of home improvement show host surveying her masterpiece. She ignored the fact that there was still an entire pile of mismatched, vaguely cursed-looking objects shoved in one corner. "Another few weeks of this, and it might actually look livable."

"Livable? This place is practically ready for a *Better Homes and Hexes* feature," Moira quipped, flopping down onto an overstuffed armchair they had dragged out of the attic earlier. The faded floral upholstery added a strange but cozy charm—if you didn't mind the faint scent of mothballs and something she optimistically described as 'antique funk.' She pulled out a chipped mug from a nearby box and held it up. "Hey, look at this. Classy or cursed?"

Kirsten, who was precariously balancing on a step stool while attempting to hang curtains, glanced down at the mug. "Definitely both," she said with a smirk. She gave the curtain rod a tug, only for it to wobble ominously. "Everything in this house has at least a fifty-percent chance of being haunted. Including that chair you're sitting on."

"If it's haunted, maybe the ghost can help us clean," Moira shot back, setting the mug down. "Or at least make us coffee."

"Great odds," Emmaline muttered, shoving a stray box aside with her foot. "Anyway, once we finish setting up, we need to focus on clearing a space in the attic for the ritual. The full moon is in a few days, and we still need supplies."

"Right," Moira said, stretching dramatically like she was about to lead a yoga class. "Let's go play in the creepy attic, because nothing ever goes wrong in an old attic. Just once, I'd like to do a ritual somewhere nice. Like a beach. Or a luxury spa. With cocktails."

Kirsten snorted from her perch on the stool. "You know we'd probably summon something that turns the spa water into cursed slime."

Moira grinned. "Fine. But I'm still voting for cocktails at the next full moon ritual."

Emmaline sighed but couldn't suppress a smile. "Let's just get through this one without summoning anything by accident first."

The attic was dimly lit by a single bulb that hung from the ceiling, casting long shadows across the room. Old trunks, dusty furniture, and stacks of yellowed newspapers filled the space, giving it the appearance of a forgotten time capsule from a century ago. Cobwebs hung in the corners, their delicate threads shimmering faintly in the weak light.

Moira took one step in and immediately sneezed. "This place smells like expired mothballs and regret," she declared, waving a hand in front of her face. "Are we sure we need to do the ritual up here? What's wrong with the perfectly fine creepy living room?"

"Don't be dramatic," Emmaline said, stepping carefully over a stack of newspapers that looked like they might disintegrate if breathed on too hard. "We just need enough room for the altar and the circle."

"Dramatic is kind of my thing," Moira replied, grabbing a broom and half-heartedly swiping at the floor. A cloud of dust rose up, making her cough violently. "Ugh, this place needs more than a broom. We need a flamethrower. Or an exorcist."

Kirsten tried to open an old window to let in some air. The window groaned in protest before slamming back down on her fingers with a loud *thunk*.

"Ow! Damn it!" Kirsten yelped, yanking her hand back and shaking it furiously. "This house is out for blood!"

"At least it's only your fingers," Moira said with a grin. "I'm expecting a ghost to pop out and offer us a cursed teapot any second."

After some effort—and several more minor mishaps, including Emmaline knocking over a stack of old books that narrowly missed Kirsten's head—the attic began to look somewhat organized. They cleared a large enough space in the middle of the room, set up the altar, and placed a few candles and crystals around it.

"Not bad," Emmaline said, wiping her hands on her jeans. "Now we just need to gather the herbs and finish preparing the spell."

"And wine," Moira added. "You can't have a proper ritual without wine."

"That's for after the ritual," Emmaline said with a pointed look.

"Details," Moira said, waving a hand dismissively. "Alright, what's next?"

Kirsten glanced at the window warily. "Next, we hope the attic doesn't collapse on us during the ritual."

Emmaline sighed again but couldn't help laughing as they made their way back downstairs, already mentally adding "attic reinforcement" to their growing list of house repairs.

By the time evening rolled around, the house felt more put together. The living room was now decorated with mismatched furniture, a few scattered books, and a rug that was only slightly frayed around the edges. The kitchen, though still in need of some serious deep cleaning, was functional enough to brew tea and warm up leftovers.

Moira emerged from her room carrying a stack of old VHS tapes she had found in the attic. "Who's up for a horror movie marathon?" she asked, holding up a tape with a faded label that read *The Fog*.

"Is that even still playable?" Kirsten asked, eyeing the tape warily.

"Only one way to find out," Moira said, popping it into the ancient VCR they had unearthed earlier.

Emmaline poured them each a glass of wine as the opening credits flickered onto the screen. "Cheers to making this house a home," she said, raising her glass.

"And to not getting cursed by any of the random junk we found," Kirsten added, clinking her glass against Emmaline's.

"I'll drink to that," Moira said, settling onto the couch.

As the movie started, the eerie voice of the old man telling a group of kids a ghost story, accompanied by the sound of a crackling campfire, set the ominous tone of the movie. filling the room with an unsettling tension.

"God, I love this movie," Moira said, leaning forward with wide eyes. "Adrienne Barbeau is such a queen."

"Adrienne and Jamie Lee Curtis in one movie? Honestly, iconic," Kirsten added, stuffing a handful of popcorn into her mouth.

"I forgot how creepy this is," Kirsten said between bites. "I swear this fog looks more realistic than what they use in modern movies."

"Right? And it's actual fog, not some CGI nonsense," Emmaline added, her eyes glued to the screen. The pale, creeping mist on the screen seemed to seep into the living room, adding an extra layer of eeriness.

The sound of footsteps on wet cobblestones echoed from the TV, accompanied by the distant tolling of a bell. As the camera panned across the deserted town, shrouded in fog, all three witches fell silent, absorbed in the growing tension.

When a ghostly figure appeared suddenly in the fog, wielding a hook, Moira shrieked and nearly spilled her wine.

"You okay there, drama queen?" Kirsten teased, reaching over to steady Moira's glass.

"Shut up," Moira whispered, clutching a pillow to her chest. "That guy just popped out of nowhere!"

Emmaline chuckled but soon grew quiet as the tension in the movie mounted. The fog on the screen grew thicker, enveloping the helpless townspeople. The sound of waves crashing against rocks and the haunting moan of the foghorn created an almost claustrophobic atmosphere in the room.

"This part always gives me chills," Emmaline said quietly as the camera showed the ominous silhouette of the lighthouse against the foggy night sky.

"If fog ever starts rolling in here, I'm grabbing my stuff and running," Kirsten muttered, glancing toward the window.

Just as Moira was about to respond, a loud *thud* echoed from outside, making all three of them jump. Moira nearly launched her popcorn across the room.

"What the hell was that?" Kirsten whispered, setting her glass down and peering toward the window.

Emmaline frowned, already heading toward the front door. "Stay here. I'll check it out."

"Like hell you will," Moira said, grabbing a flashlight and following her. "If this is how we die, we die together."

Kirsten rolled her eyes but grabbed a heavy candlestick for good measure. "Fine. Let's go be the idiots in a horror movie."

They stepped onto the porch, the cool night air sending a slight chill through the air. The yard was bathed in pale moonlight, casting long shadows across the grass. For a moment, everything was still—too still.

Then they saw movement near the edge of the property. A figure darted away from the house, disappearing into the shadows of the trees.

"Hey!" Emmaline called out, but the figure didn't stop.

Moira shined the flashlight in the direction they had fled, but it was too late. Whoever it was had vanished into the night.

"Spying on us," Kirsten muttered, her grip tightening on the candlestick. "Great. Just what we needed."

"Think it was one of the locals?" Moira asked, lowering the flashlight.

"Probably," Emmaline said with a sigh. "We knew people were curious, but I didn't expect someone to actually sneak onto the property."

"Guess we should've expected it," Kirsten said. "New people, creepy old house—it's practically a small-town invitation for snooping."

Emmaline turned back toward the house. "Let's get inside. No point standing out here. We'll figure out what to do in the morning."

As they settled back into the living room, the earlier lightheartedness had dimmed, replaced by an uneasy tension. The haunting sounds of *The Fog* continued to play in the background, but none of them were really paying attention anymore.

"Welcome to small town life," Moira said dryly, raising her glass in a mock toast. "Home of friendly neighbors and midnight peeping Toms."

Kirsten chuckled softly, though her eyes remained on the window.

CHAPTER 12

Henry Voss wasn't exactly a well-loved figure in town, but he was known. If there was one thing the locals agreed on, it was that Henry had a knack for being in places he shouldn't be. He wasn't a criminal—at least, not in any way that would warrant a police record—but he was definitely...odd. In a town where everybody knew everybody, Henry stood out, not because he was loud or obnoxious, but because he always seemed to be lurking.

Henry was in his mid-thirties, with a wiry build and pale skin that looked as though it had never seen a proper day in the sun. His dark hair was perpetually tousled, and his brown eyes had a way of shifting nervously, as if he were constantly scanning for something only he could see. He worked part-time at the local hardware store, primarily because his uncle owned it and felt sorry for him. Customers tolerated him, but only just.

"You need anything else?" Henry would ask in a voice that was always a bit too quiet, his hands fidgeting with a loose thread on his flannel shirt. Most people didn't stick around long enough to chat.

When he wasn't stocking shelves or sweeping the floor at the hardware store, Henry spent most of his time wandering the outskirts of town. He had a fascination with old buildings and abandoned places, and he knew every nook and cranny of Albany. That's how he found himself outside the Pritchard house on a couple of previous nights, crouching behind a tree and peering through the windows.

To Henry, the Pritchard house was a mystery waiting to be unraveled. He had been obsessed with it since he was a kid, back when old Mr. Granger lived there and people whispered about ghosts, murders, and hidden treasures. When the women moved in—though he didn't know they were witches, just that they were newcomers—his curiosity skyrocketed.

"Why now?" Henry muttered to himself as he watched the flickering light from their living room window. "Why move into the Pritchard house after all these years?"

It wasn't malicious intent that drove him to spy on them. It was something deeper—a need to understand, to know what was going on in the town he had never left but always felt slightly apart from. Henry felt invisible most of the time, like a ghost walking among the living, and he figured that made him uniquely qualified to keep an eye on things.

The morning after his nocturnal excursion, Henry was back at the hardware store, rearranging a display of garden tools that didn't need rearranging. His uncle, Carl Voss, stood behind the counter, a grizzled man with a permanent scowl and a voice like nails grating concrete.

"You look like you didn't sleep," Carl said, eyeing Henry. "What were you up to last night?"

"Nothing," Henry replied quickly, too quickly. He focused intently on the rake he was holding, pretending to inspect it for flaws.

Carl grunted. "You're always up to nothing. That's the problem."

Henry didn't respond. He knew better than to engage when Carl was in one of his moods. Instead, he carried the rake to the back of the store and pretended to be busy. His mind, however, was elsewhere—on the Pritchard house and the women who had moved in.

"They seemed normal enough," he thought, recalling the brief glimpses he had caught of them through the various windows. They had been watching a movie, laughing, drinking wine. Nothing suspicious about that. But still, something about the whole situation didn't sit right with him.

Later that afternoon, Henry found himself at Ruby's Diner. The scent of frying bacon mingled with the rich aroma of freshly brewed coffee, creating a warm, inviting atmosphere. Locals filled the booths and counter stools, exchanging the usual small-town gossip over plates of eggs and hash browns.

Henry sat at the counter, cradling a cup of coffee and straining to catch snippets of nearby conversations. He didn't have to wait long.

"Did you hear about the new folks up at the old Pritchard place?" Joe's companion, an older man with a stocky build, said, leaning in slightly as if the words were somehow forbidden.

Joe answered, rubbing his chin in that slow, thoughtful way he often did. "Been working up there since they moved in. They keep me busy, that's for sure. Nobody's lived there in decades.'"

Henry perked up, leaning slightly closer to hear better.

"They seem alright," Joe continued. "Mabel invited them to the barbecue last week. Nice enough, but...I don't know. Haven't been able to get a good bead on them yet."

"It's just the Pritchard house," Mabel said dismissively, as she took her seat next to Joe. "That place gives everyone the creeps. Probably why nobody stuck around long enough to fix it up."

Henry frowned, his fingers drumming nervously on the counter. He knew the Pritchard house had a reputation, but hearing the locals talk about it made his unease grow. Maybe there was more to it than he had thought.

Ruby herself bustled over, refilling Henry's coffee with a warm smile. "You alright, Henry? You look a bit pale."

"I'm fine," he muttered, offering her a weak smile. "Just didn't sleep well."

"You oughta get some rest," Ruby said kindly. "You spend too much time worrying about things that ain't your business."

Henry knew she meant well, but her words stung more than he cared to admit. He wasn't trying to be nosy; he just wanted to understand. Was that so wrong?

As the day wore on, Henry couldn't shake the feeling that something was coming—something big. He didn't know what, but he could feel it in his bones. And if nobody else in town was going to pay attention, he would. Even if they thought he was just the odd guy who worked at the hardware store and kept to himself.

That night, as he lay in bed staring at the cracked ceiling, Henry made a decision. He would keep watching the Pritchard house. Not because he wanted to spy, but because he needed answers. Something about those women wasn't adding up, and he wasn't about to ignore his instincts.

"Just gotta be careful this time," he muttered to himself. "Don't want them catching me again."

With that, he rolled over and closed his eyes, though sleep wouldn't come easy. The mansion loomed large in his mind, a puzzle he was determined to solve.

CHAPTER 13

The late morning sun hung low in the sky, casting a golden sheen across the sprawling grounds of the old Pritchard place. The air smelled of freshly cut grass and damp earth, mingling with the faint aroma of pine from the nearby woods. Joe Wilkes, dressed in worn jeans and a flannel shirt rolled up at the sleeves, wiped a bead of sweat from his brow as he surveyed the yard.

"Alright, Clay, you take care of that busted fence by the back garden," Joe said, nodding toward the crooked wooden slats. "Jeremy, you and I will start on clearing out those overgrown hedges by the side of the house. Can't have the girls tripping over roots every time they step outside."

Clay grabbed a hammer and nails from the back of the truck. His dark hair curled slightly at the ends, broad-shouldered, with calloused hands that hinted at a life spent doing hard labor. His easy grin rarely left his face, especially when Moira came to mind.

"You know, Uncle Joe, I'm starting to see why some folks say this place is haunted," he said lightly, though his gaze lingered on the house longer than necessary—specifically on the window where Moira had been earlier.

"Haunted or not, it's a job," Joe replied, nodding toward the fence. "You can admire the ghosts later. For now, get that fence patched."

Clay shrugged and grinned, though his thoughts remained on Moira. Sure, she was sharp-tongued and probably out of his league, but there was something about her that kept him intrigued.

Jeremy, quieter and more reserved, gave a shrug as he hefted a pair of hedge clippers. "They're paying us, aren't they? Better than sitting around town doing nothing."

Joe chuckled, clapping Jeremy on the shoulder. "That's the spirit. Come on, let's get to it."

The three men worked steadily through the morning, exchanging occasional banter to pass the time.

"Hey, Jeremy," Clay said teasingly, wiping sweat from his brow, "how much you wanna bet those girls are up to something weird tonight?"

Jeremy, who was carefully clipping a thick hedge, glanced over with a smirk. "Up to something weird? That's like saying water's wet. They're witches, Clay. Weird is their job."

Joe chuckled from where he stood inspecting a patch of loose shingles. "Leave them be. Those girls aren't witches. Even if they are, it doesn't matter as long as they pay us and don't summon anything that eats us."

Clay grinned, still teasing Jeremy "Fair enough. Still, you gotta admit, it's not every day you end up working for three witches in a creepy old house."

"Could be worse," Jeremy said, shrugging. "We could be fixing up Mr. Hargrave's barn again. Remember the rats?"

"Don't remind me," Clay muttered, grimacing. "I'm still having nightmares about those things."

Joe shook his head with a chuckle. "Alright, enough chit-chat. Let's finish up this side before sundown."

Meanwhile, Emmaline, Moira, and Kirsten had driven to a neighboring town, as Albany was practically bare of shops beyond Ruby's Diner and the hardware store. The trip was necessary to gather supplies for the upcoming ritual. The main street of the neighboring town was bustling with activity, lined with small shops offering a variety of goods. The scent of freshly baked bread mingled with the aroma of roasted coffee from a nearby café, creating a welcoming atmosphere.

"Okay, we need candles, sage, and... what else?" Emmaline asked, glancing at the list in her hand.

"Charcoal, salt, and wine," Kirsten added, ticking off items on her mental checklist.

Moira grinned as they passed by a thrift store. "And maybe some better furniture for that creepy attic. I swear, if I stub my toe on one more broken chair leg, I'm moving out."

"You're not moving out," Emmaline said, rolling her eyes. "Let's just focus on getting what we need. The full moon's tomorrow, and we can't afford to mess this up."

"Fine, but I'm stopping for a coffee after this," Moira said, tossing her hair over her shoulder. "If I have to deal with any more curious stares from these towns-folk, I'm going to need caffeine."

The trio made their way through a well-stocked general store, picking up their supplies while dodging the occasional side-eye from curious locals. The cashier, an older woman with tightly curled gray hair, eyed them suspiciously but didn't say anything as she rang up their items.

"Thanks," Emmaline said curtly, grabbing the bag and heading for the door.

"Friendly bunch, aren't they?" Moira muttered as they stepped outside.

"It's a small town," Kirsten said with a shrug. "They'll either get used to us, or they'll keep staring. Either way, who cares?"

By the time they returned to the Pritchard place, the sun was beginning its slow descent toward the horizon, casting long shadows across the yard. The air had cooled slightly, and a soft orange glow bathed the landscape.

Joe, Clay, and Jeremy were still hard at work. Clay had finished fixing the fence and was now helping Jeremy clear out the last of the hedges. Joe, meanwhile, was inspecting a few loose shingles on the side of the house when he caught sight of something out of the corner of his eye.

It was a figure crouched behind the tree line, barely visible through the dense underbrush. Joe squinted, recognizing the familiar wiry frame of Henry Voss.

"What the hell..." Joe muttered under his breath. He climbed down from the ladder quietly, making his way toward the trees without alerting the others.

Henry, oblivious to Joe's approach, was peering intently through the foliage, his eyes fixed on the house. His heart was pounding, a mixture of nerves and curiosity keeping him rooted to the spot.

Why are they back so late? Henry thought. *And what are those guys still doing here?* He hadn't expected the men to still be working, and it was throwing off his plan to sneak a closer look.

Suddenly, a rough hand grabbed the back of his shirt collar, yanking him upright.

"Caught you, you little sneak," Joe growled, dragging Henry out from behind the bushes.

"Hey! Let go of me!" Henry yelped, struggling against Joe's grip.

"Not a chance," Joe said, hauling him toward the house. "You've got some explaining to do."

By the time they reached the front door, Henry was red-faced and panting, half from exertion and half from embarrassment. Joe knocked firmly, still keeping a tight grip on Henry's collar.

Emmaline opened the door, flanked by Moira and Kirsten, all three of them looking puzzled.

"What's going on?" Emmaline asked, her eyes narrowing as she spotted Henry.

"Caught this one spying on you," Joe said, giving Henry a slight shake for emphasis. "Figured you'd want to know."

Emmaline crossed her arms, glaring at Henry. "Seriously? You were spying on us?"

"I wasn't spying," Henry mumbled, his eyes darting anywhere but at the furious women. "I was just... curious."

"Curious?" Moira repeated, raising an eyebrow. "That's what creeps say right before they get a restraining order."

Kirsten snorted, barely hiding her amusement.

"Listen," Emmaline said sharply, stepping forward. "I don't care what your excuse is. Stay off our property. Next time, we call the cops."

Joe finally released Henry, who stumbled back a few steps, his face pale.

"Go on," Joe said, jerking his head toward the road. "And don't let me catch you sneaking around here again."

Henry didn't need to be told twice. He turned and bolted, disappearing down the path toward town.

Jeremy and Clay came around from the side of the house, both looking confused.

"What was that about?" Jeremy asked, wiping sweat from his brow.

Joe sighed, shaking his head. "That was Henry Voss. Local peeping tom, always sticking his nose where it doesn't belong. Harmless, mostly, but a pain in the ass nonetheless."

Clay leaned on his shovel, smirking. "Didn't think today would end with a peeping tom chase."

"Welcome to small town life," Moira said dryly, crossing her arms. "Where even fixing up a house comes with unwanted entertainment."

Kirsten chuckled. "At least we know who to watch out for now."

Joe gave them a reassuring nod. "Don't worry about Henry. He's more bark than bite. Just keep an eye out, and if he comes back, let me know. I'll handle him."

Emmaline sighed, rubbing her temples. "Thanks, Joe. I guess we needed that heads-up."

As the sun dipped lower, casting the yard in shadows, the group dispersed—the girls heading back inside, and Joe, Clay, and Jeremy gathering their tools. Despite the unsettling interruption, the evening was calm , but there was a lingering tension in the air, as if the house itself had taken note of the day's events.

CHAPTER 14

The sun had long since set, leaving the old Pritchard place cloaked in shadows. Inside, the girls gathered in the living room, candles flickering around them and casting dark, wavering shapes on the walls. The earlier encounter with Henry had left them rattled, but they knew they couldn't afford any distractions.

"Alright," Emmaline said, placing a large, leather-bound book on the coffee table. "We have everything we need for tomorrow. All that's left is to prepare the attic, finalize the spell, and... well, procure a human sacrifice."

Moira nearly choked on her wine. "I'm sorry, what now?"

Kirsten sighed, giving Emmaline a knowing look. "We need a willing sacrifice—or at least someone who won't be missed for a few hours. It's part of the ritual. We can't summon Beelzeboob without it."

"Oh, wonderful," Moira said, setting her glass down with an exaggerated eye roll. "So, not only do we have to summon a demon with the most ridiculous name ever, but we also have to kidnap someone? This just keeps getting better."

Emmaline shot her a look. "We're not kidnapping anyone. We just need someone gullible enough to come here willingly. And that's where Kevin comes in."

"Kevin?" Moira asked, raising an eyebrow. "Sleazy Kevin who thinks he's God's gift to women?"

"Exactly," Kirsten said with a smirk. "He already has a thing for you, Moira. Just invite him over. Flirt a little, and he'll come running."

Moira groaned, throwing her head back dramatically. "Fine, but if he starts talking about his car dealership or flexing his biceps, I'm gone."

"Duly noted," Kirsten said dryly. "Now can we get back to the part where we actually summon the demon and not end up with a zombie again?"

Emmaline nodded, turning her attention back to the spellbook. "If we summon him correctly, he can give us the information we need about the old curse. This house, the land, it's all tied to something bigger. We need answers, Moira."

"And you think a demon with a name that sounds like it belongs on a cheap hot sauce bottle is going to give us those answers?" Moira asked, raising an eyebrow.

Emmaline shot her a look. "He's one of the few demons who actually knows the history of this region. If we can summon him without... complications, he'll tell us what we need to know."

Moira shrugged. "Fine. But if he starts throwing fireballs or turning people into frogs, I get to say I told you so."

"Message received," Kirsten said, her tone laced with sarcasm. "Now let's concentrate on summoning this demon without turning it into another disaster."

The girls spent the next hour going over the spell, making sure they had everything in place for the full moon ritual. Despite the tension, there was an underlying excitement in the air. They were close to uncovering something big—something that could change everything.

Meanwhile, Henry Voss was pacing back and forth in his small, cluttered living room. The single bulb hanging from the ceiling cast a dim light over the mismatched furniture and stacks of old newspapers. His heart was still racing from the encounter at the Pritchard place.

They were up to something, he thought, running a hand through his greasy hair.

Henry didn't have friends. He had acquaintances, sure—people who tolerated him out of politeness—but no one he could confide in. Most of the town thought of him as a nosy oddball, someone who was always lurking where he shouldn't be. And maybe they were right. But Henry didn't care. He was convinced that something weird was going on at the Pritchard place, and he was determined to find out what.

He paused by the window, peeking through the blinds at the empty street outside. A single streetlamp flickered in the distance, casting eerie shadows on the cracked pavement. Henry felt a shiver run down his spine.

I need proof, he thought. *If I can prove they're up to something, maybe people will finally listen to me.*

With that thought, he grabbed his old camera from the shelf and set it by the door, ready for whatever came next.

Over at Ruby's Diner, the usual evening crowd was beginning to gather. The diner was warm and inviting, with its checkered floors and red vinyl booths. The smell of frying bacon and fresh coffee filled the air, mingling with the low hum of conversation.

Joe Wilkes sat at a corner booth with Clay and Jeremy, their plates piled high with burgers and fries. Clay was mid-bite when he noticed a few familiar faces entering the diner.

"Looks like half the town's here tonight," he muttered, nodding toward the door.

Joe took a sip of his coffee, his expression thoughtful. "Makes sense. There's been a lot of talk about the Pritchard place lately. People are curious."

Jeremy leaned forward, lowering his voice. "Speaking of curious, what do you think Henry was doing out there?"

Before Joe could answer, a voice interrupted them. "Henry Voss? What's that weasel up to now?"

They turned to see Ruby, the diner's owner, standing nearby with a pot of coffee in her hand.

"Caught him snooping around the Pritchard place," Joe said, leaning back in his seat. "Dragged him out by the collar."

Ruby snorted. "Figures. That boy's been nosy since he was born. Always sticking his nose where it doesn't belong."

"Think he'll be back?" Clay asked, wiping his hands on a napkin.

"Wouldn't surprise me," Joe said. "But he won't catch anything. Those girls aren't doing anything illegal."

"Maybe not illegal," Ruby said, raising an eyebrow. "But strange? Definitely. You know how this town feels about strange things."

A few other patrons had started to listen in, their curiosity piqued.

"You talking about those new girls at the old Pritchard place?" asked Ed, a middle-aged man with a bushy mustache, from the next booth over.

Joe sighed. "Yeah. Look, they hired me and the boys to help fix up the place. They seem alright. Just... keep your noses out of it. Last thing we need is more rumors flying around."

"Rumors fly faster than pigeons in this town," Ruby said with a chuckle. "But you might be right. Let's hope Henry doesn't stir up more trouble than he already has."

As the conversation continued, the atmosphere in the diner grew more animated. The chatter of the locals filled the air, blending with the clatter of dishes and the occasional hiss of the griddle. Outside, the night deepened, but inside Ruby's Diner, the warmth and familiarity of small-town life carried on, with whispers of curiosity and intrigue swirling in every corner.

Back at the Pritchard place, the girls prepared for the night ahead, unaware of the growing buzz in town. The candles flickered, casting dancing shadows on the walls, as they laid out their supplies in the attic. Tomorrow would be a pivotal day, whether they succeeded or not.

CHAPTER 15

B y mid-afternoon, the Pritchard house buzzed with quiet energy. The mismatched furniture in the living room sat in semi-organized disarray, while the scent of sage still lingered faintly in the air from Kirsten's earlier smudging session—which had produced far more smoke than anyone had anticipated. A soft breeze filtered through the cracked windowpanes, stirring the edges of an old, faded curtain as the three women gathered to finalize their plans.

"We have everything we need for tonight," Emmaline said, pacing back and forth across the creaky wooden floor. The large, leather-bound spellbook lay open on the coffee table, its yellowed pages filled with ancient symbols and barely legible handwritten notes. "All that's left is to, well... procure Kevin."

Moira, sprawled across the worn couch with her feet propped up on the armrest, raised an eyebrow. "You make it sound like we're borrowing a cup of sugar from a neighbor. We're talking about luring sleazy Kevin here, stabbing him, and hoping he doesn't stay dead."

"It has to be him," Kirsten said, carefully sorting through a pile of herbs on the coffee table. "He's exactly the kind of gullible, overconfident idiot who won't ask too many questions. Besides, he already has a thing for you, Moira. It'll be easy."

Moira groaned, tossing a throw pillow at Kirsten, who caught it with a grin. "Why do I always have to be the bait?"

"Because he likes you, and you're the only one who can keep a straight face around him," Emmaline said, flipping a page in the spellbook. "We can't afford for this to go wrong. If we don't summon Beelzeboob properly, who knows what might show up instead."

Moira sat up, grabbing a glass of water from the table. "Fine."

"We'll take over before you have to suffer through too much," Kirsten said with a smirk. "Just get him here and keep him entertained. We'll handle the rest."

Meanwhile, Henry was making his way through the woods that bordered the Pritchard property. The underbrush was thick, and twigs snapped under his worn boots with each careful step. Beads of sweat gathered on his brow despite the cool afternoon breeze. His heart pounded in his chest, not from exertion, but from a mixture of fear and determination.

They're planning something tonight, he thought. *Something big.*

Henry didn't know exactly what the girls were up to, but after last night's encounter and the talk around town, he was more convinced than ever that something unnatural was going on at the Pritchard place. He needed proof—real proof—if he wanted anyone to believe him.

He found a sturdy oak tree near the edge of the property and climbed it, settling himself on a thick branch that provided a clear view of the house. It was the ideal spot to set up when he came back later that night.

From this vantage point, he could see into most of the widows on this side of the house, including the attic window, the faint outlines of furniture, and any movement inside. He pulled out his old camera, adjusting the focus, practicing for the pictures he planned to capture upon his return.

I knew something was off about them, he thought, gripping the camera tightly. *Tonight, I'll find out exactly what it is.*

Over at Ruby's Diner, the usual mid-afternoon lull had settled in. The scent of fried food and fresh coffee filled the air, blending with the hum of conversation. Joe Wilkes, Clay, and Jeremy sat at their usual booth near the window, enjoying a well-deserved break.

Clay, his dark hair still slightly damp from sweat, leaned back in his seat and took a sip of sweet tea. "So, what do you think they're really up to?" he asked, glancing at Joe. "You don't think they're actually planning some kind of... witchy ritual, do you?"

Joe set his coffee mug down, the sound of ceramic against wood echoing softly. "Does it matter? They hired us to do a job, and they've paid on time. That's all we need to worry about."

Jeremy, who had been quietly picking at his fries, finally spoke up. "Still, it's weird, isn't it? I mean, who moves into a place like that and starts burning herbs and chanting stuff?"

Before Joe could respond, Ruby approached with the coffee pot, topping off their mugs. "You boys talking about those new girls again?" she asked, a knowing smile playing on her lips.

Clay chuckled, scratching the back of his neck. "Guilty. Can't help it. They're... different."

"Different doesn't mean dangerous," Ruby said, setting the pot down on the counter. "But you know how this town is. Folks love to talk, and talk turns into stories real quick."

"Like Henry," Joe said with a nod.

Ruby snorted. "That boy's been a nosy little sneak since he was knee-high. Always poking his nose where it doesn't belong. You think he'll be back?"

"Probably," Joe said. "But he won't find anything. Those girls might be strange, but they haven't done anything wrong."

Ed, a middle-aged man with a thin mustache sitting at the next booth, leaned over. "You really think they're witches?" he asked, his tone half-joking, half-curious.

"Does it matter?" Joe repeated, glancing at Ed. "They're not hurting anyone. Let 'em be."

Ruby chuckled, wiping her hands on her apron. "You know how people are, Joe. If it's different, it's scary. But as long as they keep to themselves, I don't see the harm."

Jeremy shrugged, finishing off the last of his fries. "Let's just hope Henry doesn't stir up more trouble. Last thing we need is this turning into some kind of town spectacle."

"Agreed," Joe said, tossing a few bills onto the table. "Come on, boys. Let's get back to work."

As they stood and made their way out of the diner, the conversations continued behind them. Whispers of curiosity and speculation filled the air, blending with the clatter of dishes and the hiss of the griddle.

Later that evening, Moira stood outside Ruby's Diner, smoothing down her skirt and taking a deep breath. The late afternoon sun cast a golden glow on the diner's faded sign, and the scent of fried food lingered in the air. She spotted Kevin leaning casually against his flashy red convertible, chatting with a couple of locals. His shirt was unbuttoned just enough to show off his gaudy gold chain resting on his chest, and he wore the same smug expression he always seemed to have.

"Alright, Moira," she muttered to herself. "Just get through this without puking."

With her best attempt at a charming smile, she sauntered over. "Hey, Kevin," she said, her voice a touch too sweet.

Kevin turned, his eyes lighting up as they landed on her. His grin widened into something he probably thought was irresistible. "Moira! Well, this is a surprise. What can I do for you, gorgeous?"

Inwardly, Moira cringed, but she kept her composure. "I was wondering if you wanted to come by the old Pritchard place tonight. We're having a... gathering. Thought you might want to join us."

Kevin's eyes gleamed with interest, though not for the reasons Moira had hoped. He immediately assumed this was his lucky day. She's totally into me, he thought smugly. Why else would she invite me to that creepy old house? He leaned in slightly, lowering his voice as if they were sharing a secret. "A gathering, huh? Sounds intriguing. You know, I've always wanted to get a look inside that place." He flashed another grin. "And, of course, I'd never pass up an invitation from you."

Moira forced herself to keep smiling, though it felt more like baring her teeth. "Great," she said, her tone flat but polite. "Come by around eight."

"I'll be there," Kevin said, grinning like he had just won the lottery, giving her what he probably thought was a seductive wink. As Moira turned on her heel and walked away, resisting the urge to shudder. "This better work," she muttered under her breath.

Kevin watched her walk away, already picturing how the night would go. This is gonna be wild.

CHAPTER 16

By the time the sun set, the Pritchard house was bathed in shadows, the pale light of the moon casting an eerie glow over the property. Inside, the girls were busy preparing for the ritual.

"Alright, everything's set," Emmaline said, arranging the candles in a circle. "Where's Moira?"

"Right here," Moira said, walking in with a bottle of wine. "He's on his way. I hope you two are ready, because I deserve hazard pay for putting up with him."

"Relax," Kirsten said with a grin. "This is going to go perfectly."

"You mean like last time?" Moira shot back, raising an eyebrow. "The time we almost summoned a demon goat instead of an actual demon?"

Emmaline winced. "We've learned from our mistakes. This time will be different."

Just as she finished speaking, there was a knock at the door.

"Showtime," Moira muttered, setting the wine down and heading for the door.

She opened it to find Kevin Rawlins standing on the porch, flashing his usual overly confident grin. He had gone all out for the evening, clearly under the impression that this was some kind of *exclusive* invitation. His shirt—unbuttoned one too many buttons—revealed his standard gaudy gold chain resting against his tanned chest. His cologne was overwhelming, as if he had taken a full-body dip in a vat of it.

"Hey, ladies," Kevin said, leaning against the doorframe. "Ready to party?"

Moira resisted the urge to groan. *This is for the ritual. This is for the ritual.*

"Come on in," she said, stepping aside.

Kevin sauntered inside, looking around with a mix of curiosity and amusement. "Wow, this place is... unique." His eyes lingered on the flickering candles, the chalk-drawn symbols on the floor, and the assortment of jars filled with herbs, bones, and other strange objects.

"It has character," Kirsten said smoothly. "Come on, we've got something special planned."

Kevin smirked, clearly misunderstanding. "Oh, I *bet* you do."

Moira rolled her eyes behind his back.

As Kevin followed them deeper into the house, he couldn't help but smirk. *Tonight's gonna be unforgettable.*

Henry, perched in the sturdy limbs of an old oak tree just beyond the Pritchard house, his heart thudding in his chest with an uneasy rhythm. The air was thick with the scent of damp earth and pine needles, and the pale light of the rising moon illuminated the sprawling grounds below. From his vantage point, Henry had a clear view of the attic window, where flickering candlelight cast eerie shadows against the warped glass panes.

He shifted slightly, trying to steady himself on the branch. His curiosity had driven him here, but what he was seeing now went beyond mere curiosity—it bordered on fear. Through the attic window, he could make out the three women moving about, their movements deliberate and ritualistic. Then his eyes locked onto Kevin, standing awkwardly in the center of a chalk-drawn circle surrounded by candles.

"What the hell are they doing?" Henry whispered to himself, gripping the rough bark of the tree tighter.

He watched as Emmaline approached Kevin, a knife gleaming in her hand. The blade caught the candlelight, casting a brief flash that made Henry's breath hitch. His pulse quickened as he saw her raise the knife high. Henry eagerly watched the scene unfold with horrid fascination. He was so captivated by what he was seeing, he had completely forgotten the camera clutched in his hand.

"No way... they're not really—"

Before he could finish the thought, Emmaline plunged the knife downward. Henry's eyes widened in horror as Kevin collapsed to the floor. He felt a cold sweat break out across his forehead, and he nearly lost his balance on the branch.

"They killed him," he muttered, voice trembling. Panic gripped him as he scrambled down the tree, his mind racing. He stumbled when he hit the ground, heart pounding in his ears. *I knew something was off about them. They're murderers.*

Henry didn't stop to think. He took off at a run, disappearing into the shadows of the woods, determined to figure out what he had just witnessed—or to warn someone before it was too late.

The attic, dimly lit by the flickering glow of dozens of candles, smelled faintly of melted wax, bitter herbs, and the faint musk of old wood. Shadows flickered wildly on the slanted wooden walls, giving the space an unsettling, otherworldly feel. The air was thick, heavy with the charged energy of the ritual gone awry.

"Uh, guys," Moira said nervously, taking a step back from the altar. Her eyes flicked to Kevin, who stood stiffly in the middle of the chalk-drawn circle. "Is he supposed to look like that?"

Kevin, who had been standing moments ago with a smug, overly confident grin plastered on his face, now looked decidedly... unwell. His skin had turned an unsettling grayish hue, as though all the life had been drained from him in an instant. Blood trickled from the wound in his chest where Emmaline's knife still stuck, the handle jutting out awkwardly.

"I think it's stuck," Emmaline muttered, gripping the knife's handle and giving it a sharp tug. It didn't budge.

"What do you mean, it's stuck?" Kirsten hissed, glancing nervously at Kevin, who was now swaying slightly, his glassy eyes fixed somewhere above their heads. "It's a knife, not Excalibur!"

"I'm telling you, it won't come out!" Emmaline tugged harder, but the blade remained firmly embedded in Kevin's chest. "This isn't what's supposed to happen!"

Kevin let out a low, guttural moan, his head lolling to one side. He took a stumbling step forward, causing the girls to scatter like startled cats.

"Oh, great," Kirsten groaned, clutching the edge of the table for support. "We turned him into a zombie."

"Classic us," Moira muttered, throwing her hands up in exasperation. "I told you this was a bad idea! First the glitter bomb, now this."

"Okay, okay, don't panic," Emmaline said, though the tremor in her voice made it clear she was barely holding it together. She flipped frantically through the ancient spellbook, the brittle pages crackling under her fingers. "We just need to... reverse it. There's got to be a counter-spell in here somewhere."

Kevin took another shuffling step forward, the knife wobbling slightly with the movement. Blood oozed slowly down his shirt, soaking the fabric in a way that was both horrifying and absurd. His mouth opened and closed as if he were trying to say something, but all that came out was a series of guttural grunts.

"Uh, can we maybe reverse it before he tries to eat us?" Moira suggested, inching behind Kirsten for cover.

Kirsten grabbed the nearest object—a heavy brass candlestick—and held it out in front of her like a weapon. "Stay back, Kevin! Don't make me use this!"

As the girls scrambled to contain their rapidly deteriorating situation, none of them noticed the faint, flickering figure that materialized briefly in the far corner of the room. Beelzeboob, clad in a tattered cloak and sporting a pair of unimpressive, slightly crooked horns, crossed his arms and let out a long, exasperated sigh.

"Mortals," he muttered, shaking his head in mild disbelief. "Every time..."

He watched for a moment, as if contemplating whether to intervene or simply enjoy the chaos, before vanishing back into the ether with a soft *pop*.

Meanwhile, Emmaline gave the knife one last desperate yank, finally managing to pull it free with a wet *schlunk* sound. Kevin didn't seem to notice the knife's removal; he simply continued to lurch toward them, blood still streaming from the open wound in his chest.

"Well, that's... better?" Emmaline said, holding the bloodied knife awkwardly.

"Better?" Moira snapped. "He's still a zombie, and now he's a zombie with a hole in his chest! How is that better?"

Kirsten glanced at the trail of blood dripping onto the attic floor. "Uh, guys? We might want to do something before he ruins the floor. That's original wood."

"Priorities, Kirsten," Moira said, backing up further. "How about we focus on not dying first?"

Kevin stumbled forward, his eyes vacant, his movements jerky and unnatural. The three women watched in a mix of horror and disbelief as he swayed dangerously toward them.

"Uh, guys?" Moira whispered, edging toward the door. "Our zombie just went mobile."

"Maybe he's not fully... you know... zombified." Kirsten said backing further into a corner of the attic.

"Right," Moira muttered under her breath. "Because he looks *totally fine.*"

Meanwhile, Kevin let out a low, guttural groan, his head lolling to one side. Without warning, he pivoted clumsily and made a beeline—well, more of a zigzag—for the attic stairs.

"He's making a break for it!" Emmaline shouted, lunging forward. "Stop him!"

But before any of them could react, Kevin had already stumbled his way down the stairs, his unsteady footsteps echoing through the old house.

"Fantastic," Moira said, throwing her hands up. "We've officially lost our zombie."

Emmaline grabbed the spellbook from the table, flipping through its ancient pages with increasing frustration. "This is bad. Really, really bad."

"No kidding," Kirsten muttered, peering down the staircase. "What do we do now?"

"We find him," Emmaline said firmly, slamming the book shut. "Before he bites someone or starts lurching around town."

Meanwhile, in the ethereal plane hovering just beyond mortal sight, Beelzeboob watched the unfolding chaos with a diabolical smirk. His form shimmered faintly, his crooked horns barely visible in the hazy glow of the void.

Shaking his head in amused disbelief. "They summon me halfway, botch the ritual, and now they're running around after a half-dead used car salesman. Pathetic."

He reached out with one clawed hand, tracing invisible symbols in the air. With each movement, a thin trail of dark energy flickered, seeping through the veil and into the mortal world.

"I suppose I could help," Beelzeboob said, his voice dripping with mock sympathy. "But where's the fun in that?"

With a flick of his wrist, he sent a ripple of chaotic energy toward the Pritchard house. The candles inside flared momentarily before sputtering out, plunging the attic into near darkness.

Emmaline froze mid-step, clutching the spellbook tightly. "Did you see that?"

"See it? I almost got set on fire!" Moira exclaimed, patting at her dress as if expecting flames to appear.

"Beelzeboob," Kirsten muttered. "He's messing with us."

"No kidding," Emmaline said grimly. "We need to fix this fast."

Elsewhere, Henry Voss was in no such rush. He crept through the woods surrounding the Pritchard property, his heart still pounding from what he'd witnessed earlier. The image of Emmaline stabbing Kevin replayed in his mind, each time more exaggerated than the last.

"They're witches," he whispered to himself, clutching the flashlight in his trembling hand. "I knew it. Murderous witches."

He stumbled over a root, barely catching himself before he hit the ground. The forest was eerily silent, the usual chorus of crickets and frogs absent. It was as if the very woods were holding their breath, waiting.

Henry's mind raced. He needed to tell someone—*anyone*—what he had seen. But who would believe him? He had a reputation in town, and not a flattering one. Known more for his nosy nature and conspiracy theories than anything else, Henry knew people wouldn't take him seriously.

Still, he couldn't just do nothing. He had to—

Snap.

Henry froze, the sound of a breaking twig echoing unnaturally loud in the stillness. He spun around, flashlight beam dancing wildly across the trees. "Who's there?"

No answer. Just the faint rustle of leaves in the breeze.

Henry took a cautious step backward, his nerves fraying with each passing second. Suddenly, a cold gust of wind blew past him, carrying with it a faint, whispering voice. He couldn't make out the words, but the tone was unmistakably mocking.

"Hello?" he called out, his voice shaking. "I'm warning you—I've got a flashlight, and I'm not afraid to use it!"

Another whisper, closer this time.

Henry turned to run, but he didn't get far. Something—he didn't know what—wrapped around his ankle, sending him sprawling to the ground. His flashlight and camera flew from his hand, landing several feet away and casting long, twisted shadows.

He tried to scream, but the sound was lost in his throat as an unseen force dragged him backward into the darkness.

By the time Joe, Clay, and Jeremy walked into Ruby's Diner later that evening, the place was already bustling with its usual crowd. The soft hum of conversation mixed with the occasional clatter of plates and silver-ware, creating a lively small-town atmosphere.

"Evening, boys," Ruby said as they entered. "How's the work coming along up at the old Pritchard place?"

Joe shrugged, leading the group to a booth by the window. "Busy as ever. Those girls have their hands full, but they're making progress. Gotta say, though, they've got guts taking on that house."

Clay slid into the booth next to Joe, his gaze momentarily drifting toward the street outside. "Yeah, and they're doing a good job of it, too. Moira—" He caught himself, quickly looking down at the menu as if it held the secrets of the universe. "Uh, I mean, all of them are handling things pretty well."

Jeremy snickered quietly, but Ruby didn't miss a beat. She raised an eyebrow, pouring three cups of coffee and setting them down on the counter. "Moira, huh? Sounds like someone's taken a liking to one of those girls."

Clay muttered something unintelligible, earning a chuckle from Joe. "Relax, Clay," Joe said, picking up the coffee Ruby had brought over. "Nothing wrong with being friendly."

Before Clay could respond, an older man at the next table leaned over slightly, clearly having been eavesdropping. His name was Earl Thompson, a lifelong Albany resident with a penchant for sticking his nose where it didn't belong. "You boys really think it's a good idea, hanging around those girls? People talk, you know. That house ain't right."

Joe set down his cup slowly, fixing Earl with a steady look. "People talk because they've got nothing better to do. The girls are just trying to fix up the place and live their lives."

Earl didn't back down. "Maybe, but you can't deny there's something strange about them. New folks don't usually last long in that house."

Jeremy, who had been quietly sipping his coffee, finally spoke up. "Maybe they don't last because people like you won't leave them alone."

A few chuckles came from nearby tables, but Earl only grunted, clearly unhappy with the response. Ruby, sensing the conversation heading toward familiar territory, stepped in. "Come on now, Earl. Leave them girls be. They're doing just fine, and last I checked, none of us live there, so what's it to you?"

Earl muttered something under his breath and turned back to his plate, defeated for now. The conversation at the surrounding tables returned to normal, but Joe could still feel the undercurrent of unease lingering in the air.

"Thanks, Ruby," Joe said quietly, raising his cup in a small gesture of appreciation.

Ruby waved a hand dismissively. "I've lived here long enough to know when people are just looking for something to gossip about. As far as I'm concerned, those girls are braver than half the folks in this town for even stepping foot in that house."

Clay, feeling emboldened by Ruby's words, finally looked up from the menu. "They're good people," he said firmly. "And besides, whatever weird stuff might've happened at the Pritchard place before, that's got nothing to do with them."

Jeremy nodded in agreement, adding, "If anything strange happens, it's probably just because it's an old house. You know how places like that creak and groan at night."

Ruby smiled as she collected their empty plates. "Exactly. So, unless anyone's got anything more exciting to talk about than old ghost stories, let's all mind our own business."

Joe chuckled, finishing his coffee. "Couldn't have said it better myself."

As the three men paid their bill and prepared to leave, the chatter in the diner returned to lighter topics—fishing, the weather, and a rumored festival in the neighboring town. But as they stepped outside into the cool evening air, Joe couldn't help but glance toward the darkened street leading to the Pritchard house. He didn't believe in curses or ghost stories, but something about tonight felt... off.

"Let's head back," he said, pulling his jacket tighter against the chill of the damp night air. "I want to make sure everything's alright up there."

Jeremy and Clay exchanged a glance but followed without question. Whatever rumors swirled around town, they knew where their loyalties lay—with the girls at the old Pritchard place.

CHAPTER 17

Inside the Pritchard house, tension simmered beneath the surface. The ritual had gone terribly wrong, and now Kevin was missing—a zombie loose somewhere in Albany.

"This is bad," Emmaline muttered as she paced back and forth across the creaky floorboards of the living room. She gripped the ancient spellbook tightly, flipping through its brittle pages for answers that weren't there. "This is so bad."

Moira, sprawled on the couch, cradled a glass of wine and looked utterly unimpressed. "Oh, it's fine. He's only a *zombie*. It's not like that's a problem or anything."

Kirsten shot her a glare. "You're not helping."

"Well, neither is panicking," Moira retorted. She waved her glass in the air, the wine sloshing dangerously close to the rim. "For all we know, Kevin's wandering around, thinking about used cars and bad pickup lines."

"Or," Emmaline snapped, "he's thinking about *brains*." She slammed the book shut, sending a puff of dust into the air. "We have to find him before anyone notices."

Kirsten, ever the pragmatist, grabbed her jacket. "Let's split up. Moira, you're with me. Emmaline, you stay here in case he comes back."

Moira groaned. "Fine. But if he tries to eat us, you're throwing the first punch."

Meanwhile, in the woods bordering the Pritchard property, Joe, Clay, and Jeremy made their way back toward the house after their visit to Ruby's Diner. The moon hung low in the sky, casting long shadows across the leaf-strewn ground.

"Think those girls are alright?" Clay asked, breaking the silence. He shoved his hands into his jacket pockets, his eyes flicking toward the dark outline of the Pritchard house in the distance.

Joe shrugged. "They've got guts, I'll give them that. But something about tonight feels... off."

Jeremy, trailing slightly behind, frowned. "Off how? You think it's because of that Henry guy creeping around earlier?"

"Maybe," Joe said, his voice thoughtful. "Or maybe it's just this place. People have been talking about the Pritchard house being cursed for decades. Doesn't mean I believe it, but you can't deny weird things keep happening."

As they neared the edge of the property, Clay caught sight of something unusual. "Hey, wait—do you see that?" He pointed toward the base of an old oak tree near the fence line.

Joe and Jeremy followed his gaze, their eyes landing on a crumpled shape lying on the ground.

"Is that...?" Jeremy started, but his words trailed off as they moved closer.

Joe knelt down, his brow furrowing as he examined the figure. It was Henry—motionless, pale, and disturbingly still. His eyes stared blankly upward, as if frozen in fear.

"Is he dead?" Clay whispered, his voice laced with disbelief.

Joe reached out and pressed two fingers to Henry's neck, searching for a pulse. After a tense moment, he shook his head grimly. "Yeah. He's gone."

Jeremy stepped back, his face pale. "What the hell happened to him?"

Joe didn't answer right away. His eyes scanned the area, searching for any clues. There were no obvious signs of injury, no blood, nothing to indicate what had caused Henry's death. But something about the way his body was positioned—twisted, as if he'd fallen backward—set Joe on edge.

"We need to tell the girls," Joe said finally, standing up. "Whatever happened, they might have seen something."

Clay hesitated. "You don't think... they had anything to do with this, do you?"

Joe gave him a hard look. "No. But they might know what we're dealing with."

Without another word, the three of them hurried toward the house, their footsteps crunching loudly on the gravel driveway in the still night.

Back inside, Emmaline was just about to head upstairs when there was a frantic knock at the door. She exchanged a wary glance with Kirsten, who had just returned from checking the perimeter.

"Who is it?" Emmaline called out, her hand resting on the doorframe.

"It's Joe!" came the urgent reply.

Emmaline opened the door to find Joe, Clay, and Jeremy standing there, looking pale and winded.

"Something's happened," Joe said, stepping inside without waiting for an invitation. "It's Henry. We found him out by the tree line. He's dead."

Moira, who had just come down the stairs, froze in place. "Wait—*Henry's dead*?"

Kirsten frowned. "How?"

Joe shook his head. "We don't know. No injuries, no blood—just... dead."

Emmaline's mind raced, her thoughts a chaotic jumble of panic and disbelief. Henry had been spying on them earlier, and now he was dead? This wasn't a coincidence. Something was happening—something far beyond their control.

Before she could say anything, there was a sudden, chilling gust of wind that swept through the room, snuffing out the candles and leaving them in near darkness. The girls and the men exchanged uneasy glances as the temperature seemed to drop several degrees in an instant.

"Did anyone else feel that?" Clay whispered, his voice barely audible.

Emmaline tightened her grip on the spellbook. Whatever was happening, they were running out of time—and if they didn't act soon, things were only going to get worse.

CHAPTER 18

By morning, the town of Albany was buzzing like a kicked hornet's nest.

Word of Henry Voss's death had somehow managed to spread faster than a grease fire in a diner kitchen. By the time the sun crept over the horizon, folks were already gathering at Ruby's Diner, talking in hushed but urgent tones over their coffee and eggs. The usual morning crowd—farmers, shop owners, and the handful of retirees who never missed a chance to speculate about town business—had doubled in size. Even people who had no real reason to be up this early found themselves drawn to the diner, eager to hear the latest.

At the counter, Earl Thompson leaned forward, his bony elbows resting on the Formica surface as he shook his head. "I'm telling you, something ain't right about this. Henry was fine last night, and now he's dead? Just like that? It don't make sense."

"It sure don't," muttered Donnie Wells, a thickset man in his late forties who worked over at the feed store. "What'd he even die of?"

"Wasn't natural, I'll tell you that much," Earl said darkly, stirring his coffee with unnecessary force. "That house, man. That damn house."

Across the room, at one of the booths near the window, Mabel rolled her eyes. "Oh, for God's sake, Earl, you think everything's a damn conspiracy. Henry wasn't exactly the picture of health, you know. Man was always lookin' over his shoulder like he expected the devil himself to come tap him on the back."

Ruby, who had been refilling coffee cups at the counter, gave Mabel an approving nod. "Mabel's right. For all we know, the man had a heart attack. It happens."

"Heart attack?" Earl scoffed. "In the woods? Just layin' there like someone struck him dead? You ever seen a heart attack do *that*?"

The diner fell quiet for a beat, everyone shifting uncomfortably. Earl had a point, and no one really wanted to admit it.

It wasn't long before someone brought up the new residents of the Pritchard house.

"I heard Henry was pokin' around up there last night," said Sue Ellen, a woman who could be counted on to know everyone's business whether they wanted her to or not. She leaned in conspiratorially, her voice just loud enough to be overheard by the tables around her. "Snooping, like he always did. Maybe he saw something he shouldn't have."

"You mean *they* did something to him?" Donnie asked, lowering his voice.

"I'm just saying it's mighty strange," Sue Ellen replied, sipping her coffee in a way that suggested she had all the answers and was just waiting for someone to catch up. "Those girls come to town, start messing with *that house*, and now Henry drops dead?"

Murmurs rippled through the diner.

"They didn't seem like the type," Mabel said, but her voice lacked its usual conviction.

"You ever really *know* people?" Sue Ellen countered, raising an eyebrow. "Especially ones who ain't from around here?"

At that moment, the bell above the diner door jingled. Every conversation stopped dead as Joe, Clay, and Jeremy walked in. The three men, clearly not in the mood for small talk, made their way to their usual booth. Joe's expression was unreadable, but Clay's jaw was tight, and Jeremy looked like he was already regretting leaving the house that morning.

Earl was the first to break the silence. "Heard y'all were up at the Pritchard place last night."

Joe took his time pouring sugar into his coffee before answering. "We were."

Earl's eyes narrowed. "You see anything?"

"We saw Henry dead by the tree line," Joe said flatly. "That's it."

Earl didn't look convinced. "And you don't think that's *real* strange?"

Joe met his gaze evenly. "I think Henry was the kind of man who stuck his nose where it didn't belong. If he got himself into trouble, it had nothin' to do with those girls."

Sue Ellen snorted. "Please. Y'all are defendin' them like you know 'em."

"Maybe we do," Clay said, finally speaking up. His voice was calm, but there was an edge to it. "And maybe we know they had nothin' to do with Henry dyin'."

"You can't be *sure* of that," Donnie pointed out.

Jeremy leaned forward, his voice low. "We're a hell of a lot more sure than any of you standing around swapping gossip."

The tension in the diner thickened, but no one dared challenge them outright. Joe, Clay, and Jeremy weren't men to be argued with lightly, and everyone knew it.

Ruby, sensing things were about to turn ugly, clapped her hands. "Alright, that's enough of that. Unless one of you's the coroner and *knows* what killed Henry, I don't want to hear any more talk about those girls being involved. Y'all love a good ghost story, but let's not go accusing people of murder without a lick of proof."

Earl grumbled something under his breath but didn't push further.

Joe took a sip of his coffee and finally exhaled. "Thanks, Ruby."

"Don't thank me," she said. "Just don't let those girls come into town and get blindsided by a bunch of fools with torches."

The diner settled into a quieter, uneasy murmur.

Joe, Clay, and Jeremy exchanged a look. The town was stirred up, and it wasn't going to calm down anytime soon.

They had to warn the girls.

CHAPTER 19

Kevin Rawlins had always thought highly of himself.

Even now—despite the whole dying and coming back as a zombie thing—he still considered himself God's gift to women and, more importantly, the undisputed king of used car sales.

The problem was, no one seemed to appreciate his charm anymore.

For starters, he couldn't talk. Not properly, anyway. Instead of smooth-talking his way into deals (or Moira's pants), all that came out of his mouth were deep, guttural moans and the occasional wet gurgle.

It was frustrating.

Here he was, in his prime, and now he was *literally* dead weight.

But Kevin, being Kevin, was nothing if not an optimist.

So, he pressed on, determined to make the most of it.

Kevin lurched out of the woods like a cryptid caught on a security camera, making his way toward the Gas & Go, Albany's sad excuse for a convenience store.

Neon lights flickered in the distance, their glow buzzing like an invitation.

Gas stations meant snacks.

Snacks meant sustenance.

Sustenance meant...

...Wait.

What *was* sustenance again?

Kevin frowned—or tried to. His facial muscles weren't exactly cooperating. He grunted in frustration and staggered forward, his rotting limbs carrying him toward the glowing beacon of late-night bad decisions.

Inside, Todd Jenkins, the night shift clerk, was scrolling through his phone with the enthusiasm of a man who had given up on life.

He barely registered the thud against the glass.

Then came the low, wet groan.

Todd's head lifted, his soul temporarily leaving his body.

Kevin was pressed up against the window, his blood-stained face smushed against the glass like an overgrown toddler looking into a candy shop.

There was a long, awkward silence.

Kevin slowly lifted one decayed hand...

...And gave finger guns.

Todd blinked.

Then, without breaking eye contact, he pressed the LOCK DOOR button.

Kevin let out a frustrated grunt and rattled the door, confused as to why the world was suddenly against him.

Todd sighed, picked up the landline, and dialed.

"...Sheriff? Yeah, it's me. We got another meth head outside."

Kevin groaned in exasperation.

This was not how he imagined his night going.

And then—the sprinklers turned on.

Kevin barely had time to react before a jet of ice-cold water smacked him directly in the face.

The Gas & Go's motion-triggered sprinkler system had decided he was a threat that needed hydration.

Kevin flinched, stumbling backward as freezing water soaked his already ruined shirt. His half-buttoned disaster of an outfit now clung limply to his rotting frame.

And then—

With zero warning—

His left ear just... fell off.

Just plopped right onto the pavement like a discarded chicken nugget.

Kevin shrieked.

Or at least, he tried to.

What came out sounded like a drowning walrus in a blender.

Todd, from inside the store, watched the whole thing unfold with mild concern but mostly morbid fascination.

Then, without breaking eye contact, he picked up the phone again.

"Yeah, Sheriff? I don't think this one's on meth."

Kevin, humiliated, wet, and down one ear, staggered off into the night.

He needed to regroup.

Plan.

Reclaim his dignity.

Kevin was sick of being ignored.

Sick of being mistreated.

Sick of people not appreciating his greatness.

And then he saw it.

His sanctuary.

His territory.

His empire.

LEN'S AUTO SALES.

This was where he belonged.

Kevin perked up, or at least tried to. His posture was so far gone that his version of standing straight looked like a poorly-assembled scarecrow.

But no matter.

He had business to attend to.

Inside the tiny main office, Jerry McMillan, the night manager, was flipping through paperwork when he heard a noise.

At first, he ignored it.

Then the moaning started.

Then the banging on the glass.

Jerry turned.

And immediately wished he hadn't.

Kevin was pressed against the window, staring inside, looking like the world's worst promotional mascot.

And then—finger guns.

Jerry screamed.

Kevin, thinking this was a potential customer reacting to his overwhelming charm, let out a pleased grunt.

Jerry, thinking this was the start of the apocalypse, did the only logical thing:

He jumped over the desk, ran out the back door, and peeled out of the parking lot so fast his tires screeched.

Kevin blinked slowly.

Then looked around.

The lot was empty.

He was now the sole employee of Len's Auto Sales.

A smug, grotesque grin spread across his half-decayed face.

Kevin Rawlins was officially back in business.

Ten minutes later, a man in a cowboy hat pulled into the lot.

Kevin perked up.

His first sale!

The man stepped out, looking around before spotting Kevin standing in the

Office window.

"Uh… hey?" the man called. "You work here?"

Kevin nodded enthusiastically.

Which, unfortunately, caused his other ear to fall off.

The man froze.

Kevin, ever the salesman, waved his rotting arm in what he hoped was a friendly gesture.

And then, when the man hesitated, Kevin did what he did best.

He gave him the damn finger guns.

The man screamed and ran.

Kevin watched him go, disappointed.

But he refused to be discouraged.

Because tomorrow was a new day.

And Kevin Rawlins was going to sell a damn car.

Even if it killed him.

Again.

CHAPTER 20

The attic of the Pritchard house still smelled like candle wax, burnt herbs, and regret.

Moira sat at the kitchen table, staring blankly at the massive mess of ritual supplies they had abandoned after Kevin made his grand, undead escape. The chalk lines on the attic floor were still smudged with zombie blood, and someone—probably Kirsten—had left a half-eaten grilled cheese sandwich on top of the summoning book.

Everything about this screamed "bad decisions were made here."

Emmaline, arms crossed, paced back and forth while Kirsten flipped through the ancient spellbook again, muttering under her breath.

"Alright," Emmaline finally said, exhaling sharply. "Where the hell is Kevin?"

Moira snorted. "I don't know. Maybe he's working his way through the low-budget diners of Louisiana in search of his next terrible business venture."

"We can't just let him wander around town!" Kirsten argued. "He's a zombie! An *actual* zombie! And—" she hesitated, flipping another page before shooting Emmaline a guilty glance. "—technically, he's *our* responsibility."

Emmaline stopped pacing long enough to glare at her. "*Technically*?"

"Okay, fine." Kirsten sighed. "He *definitely* is. And if we don't find him, someone else will. And then they'll either shoot him, or worse—" she grimaced, "—*run tests* on him."

Moira made a face. "Oh god. I do *not* want Kevin ending up in some underground government lab."

"He'd probably enjoy the attention," Emmaline muttered. "But fine. We'll find him. Just—first, let's make sure that we haven't unintentionally made things worse."

All three of them looked around the house at the ominous silence that had settled in.

Something felt... *off.*

Moira narrowed her eyes. "Where's Beelzeboob?"

The realization hit them all at once.

And *that's* when the screaming started.

Ricky Poole considered himself a simple man.

He liked his beer cold, his football loud, and his barbecue sauce made with the kind of secret ingredient that could probably kill a small animal.

But most of all, he liked a quiet night.

Which is why, when a giant swarm of demonic squirrels came screeching down Main Street, Ricky immediately knew that tonight was not going to be a quiet night.

"*What in the fresh hell—*" he barely had time to say before the first squirrel leaped onto his shoulder and tried to eat his ear.

"AHH! GET OFF ME, YOU LITTLE DEVIL!"

He swatted wildly at the creature, but more were already upon him. His beer flew out of his hand, landing in the street with a tragic *splat.*

Chaos erupted around him as the horde of rabid, glowing-eyed squirrels descended on Albany like a biblical plague with fluffy tails.

Down the block, Ruby's Diner had barely closed for the evening before someone (probably Floyd, who never left on time) smashed through the front door screaming, "SQUIRRELS! *DEMON SQUIRRELS!*" before immediately tripping over a table and knocking over an entire pot of coffee.

Ruby, having seen some shit in her time running this diner, didn't even blink.

Instead, she reached under the counter, pulled out a shotgun, and muttered, "*Not tonight.*"

Outside, the squirrels had overtaken half the street.

They chased people into alleyways.

They commandeered a parked bicycle.

They somehow got into the fire station and triggered the alarm.

It was absolute chaos.

And standing right in the middle of it, watching the chaos with genuine amusement, was Beelzeboob.

He was perched on the roof of the town's hardware store, legs crossed, looking deeply pleased with himself. His cloak, which had once been black and menacing, now looked like it had been stolen from a second-rate Renaissance fair vendor. His horns weren't even symmetrical—one was slightly bent, and the other had a tiny bird perched on it.

But none of that mattered.

What mattered was that he was finally having some fun.

And then he spotted Ricky trying to escape down the street.

Beelzeboob grinned.

"Oh no, no, no. You don't get to leave the party early."

With a snap of his fingers, Ricky immediately lost control of his legs, his feet sliding out from under him like he had just stepped on an oil slick.

He hit the pavement hard, his entire body jerking stiffly as an invisible force took hold.

"*Wha—? WHAT IS HAPPENING?!*"

Beelzeboob lazily floated down from the roof, landing right next to Ricky, who was now awkwardly frozen in place, unable to move.

"You ever seen a puppet show?" Beelzeboob asked casually. "Because you're about to star in one."

And then—

With another snap—

Ricky's arms started moving.

On their own.

Like a marionette being controlled by a particularly evil child.

Beelzeboob hummed thoughtfully. "You know, I never get tired of watching humans panic. It's just so... *pure*."

Ricky, still flailing uncontrollably, was FORCED to dance—somewhere between the *Macarena* and what might have been an *attempt at jazz hands*.

It was deeply uncomfortable.

But also, apparently, fatal—because mid-dance, Ricky let out one last terrified scream, then dropped face-first into the pavement.

Dead.

Beelzeboob sighed, disappointed.

"Oh well," he muttered, nudging Ricky's now-limp body with his foot. "Some people just can't keep up."

And with zero remorse, he turned back to his squirrel army to continue the night's entertainment.

"Okay, this is bad," Emmaline said flatly, watching the news broadcast of the squirrel-related chaos unfolding downtown.

"Ya think?!" Moira snapped, gesturing wildly at the TV. "Our half-assed demon summoning just turned the town into a goddamn apocalyptic rodent nightmare, and Kevin is STILL MISSING!"

Kirsten, who had been scrolling through her phone, suddenly let out a low groan.

"Oh no."

Emmaline and Moira turned to her.

Kirsten held up her screen.

There, on someone's Facebook livestream, was Kevin.

Standing in a used car lot.

Wearing a tattered blazer.

Trying to sell a 1997 Honda Accord to a terri-fied-looking customer.

Moira threw up her hands.

"Of course he's selling cars. Of course."

Emmaline grabbed her keys.

"Let's go get our zombie before he closes a deal."

And with that, the girls rushed out the door, leaving behind one burning question in their wake:

How the hell were they going to explain *this* mess?

CHAPTER 21

The Pritchard House was already a disaster zone, but at this point, it didn't even rank in the top five worst things that had happened in the last twenty-four hours.

Kevin was MIA, the town was under siege by demonic squirrels, and now there was a dead guy doing the Macarena on Main Street.

And at the center of it all?

Beelzeboob.

The girls piled into Emmaline's car, tearing out of the driveway like a coven of batshit witches on a mission.

Moira, sitting shotgun, refreshed her phone for the seventh time. "Okay, so according to this *very* shaky livestream, Beelzeboob—was last seen dancing on a hardware store roof."

"Jesus," Emmaline muttered.

Kirsten, in the backseat, had both hands pressed to her temples. "Why is this our life?"

Moira clicked on the latest update. "Oh! *Update!* He's now throwing flaming squirrels at the Dollar General."

"WHAT?!"

Moira turned the screen around. Sure enough, the video showed a group of people running for their lives as tiny, on-fire squirrels launched themselves at un-suspecting customers.

"That one just took out a lawn chair display," Kirsten whispered.

Emmaline floored it.

They found Beelzeboob exactly where Moira's livestream recon had said he'd be—on the roof of the hardware store, drinking what looked like a Big Gulp and casually observing the destruction below.

"HEY!" Emmaline shouted as they stormed up the fire escape.

Beelzeboob lazily turned his head.

"Oh," he said, raising his drink in greeting. "It's you."

The girls stared.

"Is that a... cherry slushie?" Kirsten finally asked.

"Mm-hmm." Beelzeboob took a long sip through his straw.

The three women exchanged a look.

"What. The actual. Hell."

Beelzeboob sighed. "Alright, alright. You want an explanation? Fine." He flourished his hands dramatically and cleared his throat.

"I am Beelzeboob, Demon of Mischief and Minor Annoyances, Scourge of the Weak-Willed, Breaker of—"

Moira held up a finger. "Wait, wait, wait. Minor Annoyances?"

Beelzeboob scowled. "It's a very important job."

Kirsten crossed her arms. "You're a demon. Of minor annoyances."

"Yes."

"Like... what? What exactly does that entail?"

Beelzeboob sighed dramatically, setting down his Big Gulp of Evil™ before ticking off a list on his fingers.

"I make sure your Bluetooth disconnects right when your favorite song is playing."

Emmaline's eye twitched.

"I ensure your Wi-Fi signal drops to one bar just before an important email is sent."

Kirsten narrowed her eyes.

"I cause people to spill coffee on their shirts right before job interviews."

Moira gasped. "You monster."

Beelzeboob smirked. "And I rig claw machines so you never win."

A horrified silence fell over the rooftop.

"You're evil," Emmaline whispered.

"Obviously." Beelzeboob leaned back on the ledge, looking very pleased with himself.

Moira, still staring at him like he was the worst thing to ever exist, finally spoke.

"So... do we call you Beelzeboob, or...?"

He made a disgusted face. "Ugh, no. I *hate* that name. Call me Fred."

The witches blinked.

"Fred?" Kirsten repeated.

"Yeah. Fred."

"You are a literal demon," Moira said, rubbing her temples. "And your *actual* preference... is Fred?"

"Correct."

"I want to die."

Beelzeboob—Fred, apparently—shrugged. "We can arrange that."

Moira glared.

"Alright, Fred," Emmaline said through clenched teeth. "Here's the deal. We summoned you by accident. Clearly. You need to go back."

Fred laughed.

Like, full-on wheezing laughter.

"*Ohhhhh,* no, no, no, no," he said, wiping a nonexistent tear from his eye. "I just *got here.* You think I'm going back when there's so much fun to be had?"

"You killed a man!" Kirsten snapped.

"Eh." Fred waved a hand. "Honestly, Ricky's time was up."

Moira groaned. "God, I hate that this is probably true."

Emmaline took a deep breath. "Okay, look. What if we make a deal?"

Fred arched a brow. "Go on."

"We help you cause trouble somewhere else—somewhere *not* Albany—and in return, you leave the town alone."

Fred stroked his weirdly perfect goatee. "Hmm."

He looked at the fiery squirrel chaos below.

He looked at the witches.

He looked at his Big Gulp.

Then, finally, he sighed.

"Fine. But I have *conditions*."

"Of course you do," Moira muttered.

Fred grinned, his sharp teeth gleaming.

"First, I keep the squirrels."

Kirsten nearly choked. "ABSOLUTELY NOT!"

Fred pouted. "Ugh. Fine. Party poopers."

"Second," he continued, "I want a souvenir."

The girls exchanged wary looks.

"What kind of souvenir?" Emmaline asked.

Fred's grin widened.

"I want Kevin."

The rooftop went silent.

Then Moira burst out laughing.

"Oh my god. You want KEVIN?!"

"Yup."

"You're a demon, and the *thing* you want is Kevin, the sleaziest used car salesman to ever exist?"

"He's already dead," Fred said with a shrug. "Might as well put him to good use."

Moira wiped away a tear. "Oh my god, *please* take him."

"No," Emmaline snapped. "We need to fix Kevin, not send him to hell!"

Fred rolled his eyes. "Pfft. Hell? Too much work. I was thinking Vegas."

The witches blinked.

"Wait... Vegas?" Kirsten asked.

Fred beamed. "Oh yeah. Kevin and I are gonna start a show."

Moira's jaw dropped. "Oh my GOD. You're gonna turn Kevin into a Las Vegas headliner?!"

"Think about it," Fred said, eyes gleaming. "The Undead Salesman! It's brilliant."

Kirsten buried her face in her hands.

Emmaline looked exhausted.

Moira just grinned.

"Honestly?" Moira said, crossing her arms. "That's the best possible outcome for Kevin."

Fred smirked. "Glad we agree."

Emmaline let out a long, suffering sigh.

"Fine. Take Kevin. Just leave."

Fred grinned victoriously.

"Pleasure doing business with you, ladies."

And with one final snap, the squirrels disappeared, the flames vanished, and Fred popped out of existence...

...off to find his zombie sidekick.

CHAPTER 22

Kevin Rawlins, used car salesman, semi-professional flirt, and now full-time zombie, was absolutely not prepared for what was coming.

Not that he had ever been particularly *aware* of his surroundings before dying, but still—tonight was about to get weird.

Fred, formerly known as Beelzeboob, floated lazily over the town, arms crossed, staring down at the streets with mild impatience.

"Alright, where's my boy?" he muttered. "We got *business* to discuss."

He snapped his fingers, and the air shimmered ominously—the kind of unholy disturbance that would have made seasoned demonologists faint with fear.

...Instead, it knocked out the power grid to half the town and overloaded the nearest cell tower, causing everyone's phones to spontaneously call their exes.

"*Huh.*" Fred watched as lights flickered out, sirens wailed in confusion, and dozens of unfortunate souls suddenly started yelling into their phones with varying degrees of regret.

A drunk woman burst out of a dive bar shouting, "DAMN IT, CHAD, I SAID I NEVER WANTED TO HEAR FROM YOU AGAIN!"

A man on a date watched in horror as his phone dialed both his wife and his side-piece *simultaneously.*

An elderly woman threw her phone into the street and shouted, "HAROLD'S BEEN DEAD FOR FIFTEEN YEARS, WHO THE HELL JUST AN-SWERED?!"

Fred winced. "*Yikes.*"

He snapped his fingers again, fixing nothing but giving himself sunglasses because he thought it made him look cool.

"Alright, Kevin," he muttered. "Where you hiding, buddy?"

Kevin, as he shambled through the darkened streets of town, was deep in thought

Well.

As deep in thought as a rotting brain would allow.

Which, realistically, was somewhere between a concussed goldfish and a broken GPS system.

After being denied entry at the Gas & Go, failing to sell a single used car, and being rejected by every pedestrian he approached, he was starting to rethink his strategy.

He needed a new angle.

Maybe...

...maybe people weren't responding well to the blood-soaked, one-eared, moaning corpse aesthetic.

Maybe what he needed...

...was a wardrobe change.

And that's how Kevin the Zombie ended up breaking into the Goodwill at the edge of town.

Kevin stumbled through the dark thrift store, his rotting limbs barely cooperating, knocking over entire racks of clothing in search of... something.

What **was** he looking for?

Oh, right.

Kevin shuffled up to the nearest mannequin and squinted at its questionable fashion choices.

A bright red Hawaiian shirt.

A pair of cargo shorts.

And a plaid blazer on top.

Kevin groaned in approval.

THIS.

This was style.

Within minutes, Kevin was now dressed like the worst Floridian tourist imaginable—loud shirt, oversized blazer, cargo shorts, and for some reason, socks with sandals.

He stared at himself in the reflection of a nearby display case, nodding slowly.

He looked... expensive.

He looked... like someone who could sell you a used car that may or may not still have its original brakes.

Kevin was back, baby.

And that's when the store alarm blared.

Kevin screamed.

Or, well. He tried to. It came out more like a drowning walrus gargling soup.

He spun wildly, crashing into shelves, knocking over a pyramid of VHS tapes, and tripping over a pair of roller skates that had no business being in the middle of the floor.

By the time Kevin crawled out of the store window, he looked less like a businessman and more like a Muppet that had been in a bar fight.

And that's when Fred found him.

Fred floated down from the sky, landing gracefully like an absolute drama queen, and tilted his sunglasses down to inspect his new protégé.

"Ooooooh buddy," he said, grinning. "You look like a fever dream."

Kevin turned perking up at the sound of a familiar gravelly voice.

He squinted at Fred.

Fred squinted back.

There was a long, awkward silence before Kevin slowly... raised his hand...

FINGER GUNS.

Fred gasped theatrically.

"*Bro.*"

Kevin let out a wet, guttural groan, which Fred took as a sign of understanding.

"I knew I liked you," Fred said, clapping him on the back—which, unfortunately, dislodged something important from Kevin's spine.

Fred grimaced. "Eh. You don't need that."

Kevin made a sound that was somewhere between confusion and agreement.

Fred nodded approvingly.

"Alright, buddy, here's the deal," Fred said, wrapping an arm around Kevin's semi-attached shoulders. "You and me? We're partners now. We're gonna cause some mischief, and then—" he grinned, "—we're gonna take over Vegas."

Kevin's rotting brain tried to process this.

Vegas.

Bright lights.

Slot machines.

Free buffets.

Oh my god.

Kevin grunted excitedly and finger-gunned again.

Fred finger-gunned back.

This was it.

This was destiny.

Kevin and Fred the Demon—the ultimate duo.

Moira stared at her phone.

She refreshed the livestream again.

And again.

And then she put the phone down, rubbed her temples, and muttered, "We have lost complete control of this situation."

Kirsten took a deep breath and poured another glass of wine. "You *think*?"

Emmaline, sitting on the couch watching the news, pinched the bridge of her nose. "So. Just to clarify. Beelzeboob is now called Fred."

"Yup."

"And he's teaming up with Kevin."

"Yup."

"And they're going to Vegas."

"Apparently."

There was a long pause.

Then Emmaline simply took Kirsten's entire glass of wine and drank it in one go.

Moira sighed dramatically, flopping onto the couch. "Well. Guess we're going to Vegas."

CHAPTER 23

B y the time Joe Wilkes' truck rumbled up the driveway of the Pritchard House, the girls were elbow-deep in damage control mode.

Kevin was loose, Beelzeboob, *Fred,* had turned their entire plan into a Vegas-bound dumpster fire, and they were running out of ideas faster than Moira was running out of patience.

And now, they had company.

Emmaline spotted headlights through the window, groaned,"*God. Damn. It.*"

Kirsten, still in pajamas despite it being late afternoon, looked up from her notebook where she'd been frantically scribbling a counter-spell. "*What now?*"

Moira, who had been in the middle of stress-eating an entire sleeve of Oreos, peeked through the blinds and froze.

"Shit," she muttered.

"What?" Emmaline sighed, already expecting the worst.

Moira slowly turned.

"It's Clay."

Silence.

Then Kirsten—without looking up—said, "You need to stop acting like a high schooler every time he shows up."

Moira snatched up a pillow and launched it at Kirsten's head.

Unfortunately, Kirsten had been expecting this. She caught the pillow mid-air, barely breaking concentration as she flipped another page in her book.

"Nice try, loser."

Moira scowled but before she could retaliate, a knock sounded at the door.

And another one.

And then—

"Y'all better not be dead in there, because that's a real bad look right now."

Joe called out.

"Goddammit," Emmaline hissed.

"We have to answer," Moira sighed. "If we don't, they'll assume we murdered Henry."

Kirsten snorted. "Not helping."

With no other choice, Emmaline took a deep breath, plastered on a questionably friendly expression, and yanked the door open.

Joe Wilkes stood on the porch like a pissed-off father arriving to pick up his delinquent teenagers from detention.

Jeremy, standing slightly behind him, looked bored as hell, hands in his pockets, chewing on what looked like a toothpick he found in his truck.

And then there was Clay.

Standing there, grinning, all messy dark curls and broad shoulders, like he hadn't just walked into the epicenter of the stupidest supernatural disaster Albany had ever seen.

Moira absolutely refused to let herself blush.

She failed.

Joe sighed, looking past Emmaline into the house. "So. Do I even wanna know?"

Emmaline didn't blink. "No."

Joe nodded. "Thought so."

Clay leaned against the doorframe, fixing Moira with an infuriatingly charming smirk. "You doin' okay, sweetheart? Seem a little flustered."

Moira scowled immediately. "I will throw you off this porch."

Jeremy, deadpan, said, "I'd pay to see that."

Emmaline gritted her teeth. "What do y'all want?"

Joe, completely unfazed, gestured toward town. "Well, considering we're all smack in the middle of a zombie and loose demon situation, figured we'd come check in before the place either burns down or gets hit by an exorcism raid."

Moira crossed her arms. "Big assumption that we need checking on."

Joe stared her down.

Then pointed toward the backyard.

Where the grass was still burned in the shape of a pentagram.

Moira cleared her throat. "...Fair."

Joe crossed his arms, eyes sweeping over the three women, all looking suspiciously guilty.

"Alright," he said slowly. "Since we *technically* work for y'all, mind telling us what in the hell is goin' on?"

Kirsten shot Moira and Emmaline a look that clearly meant *you explain this, I quit being the responsible one today.*

Moira sighed dramatically, rubbing her face.

"Okay," she started. "The short version is..."

"We accidentally summoned a demon," Emmaline interrupted.

Moira scowled. "I was easing into that—"

"Named Beelzeboob," Kirsten added.

"Fred," Moira corrected, at the same time Clay muttered, "What the hell kinda name is Beelzeboob?"

Joe was completely deadpan. "Y'all summoned a demon."

"Accidentally," Emmaline clarified.

Jeremy, unimpressed, shifted his toothpick. "And the zombie?"

Moira shifted uncomfortably. "That was... a side effect."

Joe blinked slowly. "A side effect."

"Of trying to sacrifice someone for the ritual," Kirsten admitted.

Joe's expression didn't change. "You sacrificed someone?"

"It didn't work!" Moira said quickly. "Well, I mean, technically it did, but Kevin's just too dumb to stay dead, and Fred is out looking for him."

"Kevin?" Clay interrupted, blinking. "Kevin Rawlins?"

Jeremy let out a low whistle. "Jesus. Y'all picked the sleaziest sacrifice possible."

"We know !" all three women snapped at once.

Joe just exhaled sharply and dragged a hand down his face. "So let me get this straight."

He held up a finger. "Y'all summoned a demon."

"Yes."

Another finger. "Tried to sacrifice Kevin."

"Technically, yes."

Third finger. "Kevin is now a zombie."

"Correct."

Fourth. "And this demon—excuse me, *Fred*—is runnin' around town tryin' to find him."

Emmaline clenched her jaw. "That is also correct."

Joe stared.

Then turned around.

Walked down the porch steps.

Took off his hat, stared at the sky like he was praying for patience, and then turned back.

"Alright," he said, voice very calm. "What's the plan?"

Moira and Emmaline exchanged a glance.

"Plan A: Fix Kevin, banish Fred, and pretend this never happened."

"Alright. Plan B?"

Moira sighed. "Move to Canada and start a new life."

Joe snorted. "Y'all ain't built for the cold."

"Then Plan C is Vegas," Kirsten muttered.

Joe raised an eyebrow. "Vegas?"

"Fred and Kevin are trying to start a show," Moira grumbled.

Jeremy cackled. "Oh my god. The zombie's goin' to Vegas?"

"Apparently."

Clay, still leaning against the porch railing, gave Moira a slow, amused grin. "Guess we're all goin' to Vegas then?"

Moira groaned loudly. "I hate everything about this ."

Clay laughed. "Yeah? Think you'll hate it less if I sit next to you in the car?"

Moira gave him a murderous glare, but her blush betrayed her.

Joe sighed deeply.

"Well," he muttered, walking back up the steps, "guess we better start packing then."

CHAPTER 24

By the time morning rolled around, the town of Albany, Louisiana, was officially on edge.

Between power surges, random phone calls from exes, exploding streetlights, and—oh yeah—a literal zombie wandering around town, folks were nervous.

And nervous people in Albany did one of two things: Pray or Gossip.

Ruby's Diner was packed by mid-morning, filled with locals swapping stories, suspicions, and—because this was the South—biscuits smothered in an ungodly amount of gravy.

At the largest booth, Mabel , Albany's unofficial reigning gossip queen, was already deep into her third cup of coffee while leaning in to talk conspiratorially with her closest friends:

Bill Hardy, an ex-sheriff who still walked around like he was in   charge

Doreen Phelps, the church organist and town's leading expert on who   was going straight to Hell

Lonnie Walker, owner of the pawnshop and "guy who knew a guy" for   literally anything

Earl Richards, who had spent most of his life fishing and telling   outrageous lies about what he caught

Bill, stirring his coffee with one finger, sighed. "So. What's the latest?"

Mabel, who had been waiting for this exact moment, leaned in. "Well," she started, lowering her voice for dramatic effect, "we all know Henry Voss turned up dead as a doornail."

"Mm-hmm." Doreen nodded, judgmentally. "He had it comin'."

Lonnie, chewing loudly on a strip of bacon, squinted. "How'd they find him again?"

Mabel licked her lips, loving every second of this. "Sheriff got an anonymous tip. Found him tangled up in the woods behind the old Pritchard place."

Earl, who had spent 60 years making up stories, scoffed. "I heard he was found half-eaten."

Mabel gave him a look. "By what, Earl? Ain't been a gator 'round here in years."

Earl, without missing a beat, deadpanned, "Mysterious circumstances."

Bill, ignoring that entirely, leaned forward. "Y'all really think it was those girls?"

Mabel smirked. "Who else?"

Doreen crossed herself. "Witches. Just like I said."

Lonnie, always the skeptic, shook his head. "Come on. We don't know they had anything to do with it."

Doreen scoffed. "Oh, please. Strange things start happening right when they move in? The Pritchard house was quiet for years."

Bill, rubbing his chin, frowned. "I don't know. If they did do it, where's the body now?"

The table fell silent.

Because that was the weirdest part.

Henry had been reported dead.

But by the time the sheriff and his deputies showed up to investigate, Henry's body was gone.

Mabel, sensing the perfect moment to stir the pot, whispered, "You ever hear what they used to say about that house?"

Earl perked up. "Oh hell, I love a good ghost story."

Bill, rolling his eyes, muttered, "Here we go."

Mabel took a long sip of her coffee before placing it down dramatically.

"Back in the day," she began, "folks said that land was cursed. People went missing. Kids, mostly. Sometimes men who wandered too close at night."

Doreen shuddered.

Earl, enjoying this way too much, asked, "They ever find the bodies?"

Mabel, lowering her voice for dramatic effect, shook her head.

"Some say," she continued, "the land eats 'em. That it takes the wicked and keeps their souls. The Pritchards knew it. That's why they left."

Lonnie, ever the realist, snorted. "Or maybe they just didn't wanna live in a damn swamp."

Doreen ignored him completely. "So you're tellin' me, we got a house full of witches living on cursed land, people start dyin', and we're supposed to believe it's a coincidence?"

Nobody had a good answer for that.

And just as the silence stretched, the diners' door burst open.

A young man stumbled inside, eyes wide, face pale as a sheet.

Sheriff Tom Dawson was having a terrible day.

First, Henry turned up dead.

Then Henry turned up missing.

Then he started getting reports about a half-decomposed lunatic terrorizing the town.

Now, sitting at his desk, Tom rubbed his temples as his deputy, Carl Stevenson, tried to explain the latest ridiculous update.

"So lemme get this straight," Tom sighed. "You're telling me Kevin Rawlins is walking around town?"

Carl nodded. "Yes."

"The same Kevin Rawlins that's been missing for a couple days?"

"Yes."

"The same Kevin Rawlins that was probably supposed to be dead?"

Carl hesitated. "...Yes?"

Tom, exhausted, leaned forward. "What did he do?"

Carl, deadpan, replied, "He broke into the Goodwill and stole a Hawaiian shirt."

Tom blinked.

Then blinked again.

Carl shifted uncomfortably. "And, uh... he might've also, uh... scared the hell out of the night manager at Len's Auto Sales."

"How?"

Carl cleared his throat. "He, uh... walked up to the window, pressed his face against it, and then just—" Carl mimed finger guns.

Tom stared.

Carl stared back.

Finally, Tom sighed. "Jesus Christ."

Then his phone rang.

With zero enthusiasm, he answered.

"Sheriff."

The voice on the other end was Ruby.

"Tom, you better get down here," she said. "There's a boy in my diner talking about a zombie in a Hawaiian shirt."

Tom closed his eyes and prayed for patience.

"I'll be right there," he muttered.

Hanging up, he grabbed his hat and looked at Carl. "Get in the car."

"Where we going?"

"To see if the town's finally lost its goddamn mind."

The entire restaurant was staring at the wide-eyed kid who had just stumbled in.

Mabel leaned forward. "What happened, son?"

The boy gulped. "I—I saw something."

Earl, excitedly, whispered, "Was it a ghost?"

The boy shook his head frantically.

"No." He swallowed hard. "It was—it was a *man.*"

Mabel squinted. "Who?"

The boy trembled.

"Kevin Rawlins."

Silence.

Doreen crossed herself again.

Earl muttered, "Well, shit."

And just as Ruby turned to grab a fresh pot of coffee, Sheriff Tom Dawson walked in.

He looked tired.

And deeply unamused.

"Alright," he said, scanning the room, "someone start talking."

Because if one more person told him a zombie was running loose, he was gonna need a drink.

CHAPTER 25

Sheriff Tom Dawson had seen a lot of strange things in his time.

Drunks streaking naked through Main Street? Check.

That one time Earl Richards swore up and down that a UFO landed in his backyard but it turned out to be Lonnie Walker's drone? Check.

A rotting used car salesman in a stolen Hawaiian shirt shambling around town terrorizing gas station clerks?

That was new.

And he did not have the patience for it.

Tom stood at the counter of Ruby's Diner, arms crossed, glowering as half the damn town sat crammed into booths, all talking over each other.

At the front of it all was Mabel , self-appointed speaker of the people, her hands clasped over her coffee cup like she was leading Sunday prayer.

"Tom," she said, in her usual 'this is serious business' voice, "you need to do something."

Tom sighed, rubbing his temples. "Do something about *what*, exactly?"

"The zombie," Mabel deadpanned.

Tom looked around. "Does anyone have any actual *proof* that Kevin Rawlins is a zombie?"

Earl Richards, who had lived six decades purely off of exaggeration and beer, raised a hand. "I saw 'im outside the Gas and Go. His ear fell off."

Tom stared. "His... *ear?*"

Earl nodded gravely. "It plopped right off like a badly fried hushpuppy."

"Jesus Christ."

Ruby, who had been listening quietly from behind the counter, spoke up. "He scared the hell outta my cook this morning."

Tom sighed. "Did he *hurt* anybody?"

"No, but he did finger guns at a priest over at the pharmacy and then tried to buy a bottle of Old Spice with Monopoly money."

Tom exhaled sharply.

"Alright, let's say, *hypothetically*, Kevin is somehow alive again—"

Mabel interrupted immediately. "Oh, he's alive, Tom. But he ain't right."

Doreen Phelps, church organist, nodded solemnly. "It's the devil's work."

Lonnie Walker, leaning against the counter, snorted. "Maybe it's just Kevin being Kevin. He always looked like he was half-decomposed anyway."

Earl raised a hand again. "His ear fell off, Lonnie."

Tom dragged a hand down his face.

He turned to his deputy, Carl Stevenson, who had been sitting silently, drinking coffee and pretending he wasn't part of this nonsense.

"Carl," Tom said.

Carl, without looking up from his coffee, sighed. "Yeah, boss?"

Tom took a deep breath.

"Find Kevin."

Carl nodded, took one last sip, and headed for the door.

Jerry McMillan, night manager, had not slept.

Not after what happened last night.

He had been closing up shop when Kevin Rawlins—in all his undead, rotting glory—walked up to the office like he still worked there, pressed his half-decomposed face against the glass, and finger-gunned him.

Jerry had screamed like a banshee, jumped the desk, and ran out the back door so fast he nearly dislocated a knee.

And now?

Now, he refused to go anywhere near the dealership.

Instead, he was at his cousin Randy's house, holed up like a doomsday prepper while trying to convince himself he hadn't seen what he *knew* he saw.

"Maybe it was a meth head," Randy offered, cracking open a Coors Light.

Jerry shot him a wild-eyed glare. "Randy. His ear fell off."

Randy paused. "Okay, but—"

"His. Ear. Fell. Off."

Randy took a long sip of his beer and muttered, "Alright, fair point."

Back at the sheriff's office, Tom was still sorting through witness reports that sounded more like rejected horror movie plots.

Kevin spotted at the Waffle House.

Kevin spotted at the library (trying to check out a copy of "How to   Win Friends and Influence People").

Kevin spotted at the Dollar General, aggressively sniffing the   candle aisle.

Tom rubbed his temples.

"This is the dumbest goddamn thing I've ever dealt with."

Then, the phone rang.

He answered gruffly. "Sheriff Dawson."

The voice on the other end was Pastor Jim Carver, nervous as hell.

"Sheriff... I think I need to report a crime."

Tom frowned. "What crime?"

A deep breath. Then:

"*...The Pritchard girls kidnapped the Devil.*"

Tom stared.

Pastor Jim continued, voice dead serious.

"I saw him. At the park. He had horns, a black robe, and was carrying a Slushie from the 7-Eleven."

Tom, officially done, slammed the phone down.

Then, after a long pause, picked it back up.

And called his deputy.

Carl answered on the first ring. "Yeah, boss?"

"...Find Kevin. NOW."

As news continued to spread, the diner turned into a war zone of opinions.

Some, like Doreen, were adamant. "The girls need to be run out of town."

Others, like Lonnie, were amused. "Let 'em stay. This is the most excitement Albany's had in years."

Ruby, ever the pragmatist, sighed and said, "I *don't care* what's going on, I just want my damn diner back."

And then, just as the yelling reached its peak—

The doors swung open.

Everyone turned.

And standing there, in all his undead, rotting glory, was...

Kevin.

In a Hawaiian shirt.

Holding a half-eaten corn dog.

And, after a long awkward silence, he slowly raised a hand...

And gave the entire diner finger guns.

Doreen screamed.

Ruby dropped a plate.

Mabel gasped, clutching her pearls like she was about to faint.

And Sheriff Tom Dawson, who had just walked in behind him, looked up at the ceiling like he was begging God to just end it all.

"...I hate this town," he muttered.

CHAPTER 26

Sheriff Tom Dawson had officially had it.

Had it with the rumors.

Had it with the panic.

Had it with Kevin Rawlins shambling through town like some kind of half-baked Scooby-Doo villain.

And now, just when he thought this day couldn't get worse—

Henry Voss's corpse had the absolute audacity to turn up again.

Alive.

Well.

Sort of.

The entire diner was frozen in horror as Kevin Rawlins—dead man walking, corn dog in hand—stood there in his cheap Hawaiian shirt, soaking in the attention like he was a goddamn celebrity.

Sheriff Dawson, who had just walked in behind him, sighed so hard his soul nearly left his body.

"Kevin," Tom said slowly, rubbing his temples. "What in the hell are you doin'?"

Kevin turned his rotting head toward him painfully slow, blinking one good eye and one unsettlingly loose one.

He opened his mouth—

And let out the most ungodly wet gurgle imaginable.

Todd Jenkins, the night clerk from the Gas & Go, who had been at a nearby table eating, turned pale.

"Nope."

Todd stood up immediately, threw cash on the counter, and walked straight out the door.

Kevin, still chewing his corn dog, raised a hand and, in classic Kevin fashion, finger-gunned the entire diner again.

The diner collectively lost its shit.

Mabel crossed herself.

Doreen fainted.

Earl Richards muttered something about the end times.

And Ruby?

Ruby just walked straight into the kitchen and started pouring whiskey into the coffee pot.

Tom clenched his jaw. "*Alright, that's it.*"

"Kevin," Tom said, gritting his teeth. "*You're comin' with me.*"

Kevin blinked.

Then, sensing he was being scolded, he shook his head.

Tom exhaled sharply. "*Kevin.*"

Kevin made a low groaning sound, took one big bite of his corn dog, and turned for the door.

"Kevin—*don't you dare—*"

Kevin dared.

He bolted.

Well.

Bolted is a *strong* word.

It was more like a slow, lumbering shamble, but still—he made a break for it.

Tom, tired and fed up, shouted, "*Get him!*"

Carl Stevenson, who was outside leaning against the patrol car, looked up just in time to see Kevin waddling at full zombie speed toward the road.

Carl frowned. "*Oh, for fu—*"

While Kevin's dramatic escape attempt was happening, Deputy Mark Holloway was having a very bad morning at the town's backwoods hunting ground.

Mark had been sent to check on a report—

Something about "a body".

Which, honestly, wasn't unusual.

People always mistook dead deer for human corpses out here.

But the moment he stepped out of the car and saw what was actually waiting for him—

He immediately wished he'd called in sick.

Laying half-covered in leaves, clothes torn, skin pale as death, was—

Henry. Fucking. Voss.

Mark stared.

Then Henry twitched.

Mark's soul left his body.

Then Henry sat up.

Mark nearly passed out.

Then Henry opened his mouth—

And hissed.

"JESUS CHRIST—"

Mark screamed, tripped over his own boots, and fell on his ass.

Henry, full-on zombified, slowly turned his head toward Mark, his jaw hanging loose like it had unhinged a little too much.

Mark scrambled backward. "Henry?"

Henry groaned.

Mark blinked rapidly, trying to make sense of what he was seeing.

"Henry, what the hell happened to you?"

Henry blinked both eyes out of sync, his body swaying like a drunk in a hurricane.

Then, without warning—

Henry lunged.

Mark screamed again, grabbed his baton, and swung wildly.

The baton smacked Henry directly in the face, sending him toppling backward into the dirt.

Mark, panting, stared down at him.

"*Oh, hell no.*"

Reaching for his radio, he pressed the button so hard he nearly cracked it.

"TOM!"

Static.

Then:

"...Yeah?"

Mark, absolutely done with life, exhaled.

"Henry Voss is alive."

Silence.

Then:

"...Excuse me?"

"*He's A GODDAMN ZOMBIE, Tom !*"

Silence.

Then:

"Fuck."

Mark nodded to himself. "Yeah. That about sums it up."

Tom Dawson was already sprinting after Kevin when Mark's voice crackled over the radio.

"Tom. Henry's back."

Tom, grabbing Kevin by the collar and yanking him back mid-limp, froze.

"Say again?"

"Henry's back. And he's trying to EAT me."

Tom closed his eyes.

Breathed in.

Breathed out.

Then, in the most defeated tone imaginable—

"Goddammit."

Kevin, not understanding why everyone was upset, offered him the last bite of his corn dog.

Tom slapped it out of his hand.

"Carl, get Kevin in the car. Mark, STAY WHERE YOU ARE."

Carl, having finally caught up, grabbed Kevin by the arm, muttering, "This is the dumbest arrest I've ever made."

Kevin, pouting, let himself be led away.

Tom, exhausted, pinched the bridge of his nose and muttered:

"What in the actual hell is happening to my town?"

CHAPTER 27

Sheriff Tom Dawson had officially hit his breaking point.

One zombie used car salesman in Hawaiian print?

Fine.

One zombified local pervert trying to eat his deputy?

Not fine.

Both of them on his hands at the same time?

Absolutely not fine.

And to top it all off?

Kevin kept humming.

Not a full song.

Not actual words.

Just a low, garbled, wet-sounding hum as he sat in the back of the patrol car like this was a joyride instead of an arrest.

Deputy Mark Holloway was having the worst experience of his goddamn life.

He had been staring at Henry Voss's undead, twitchy-ass body for the past ten minutes, trying to decide if:

A) He was hallucinating from lack of sleep.

B) Henry was about to try eating him again.

C) He should just shoot him and call it a day.

Henry, still facedown in the dirt where Mark had knocked him, gave a low, grumbling groan.

Mark flinched.

Then—with all the grace of a malfunctioning animatronic— Henry slowly sat up.

His neck cracked in a way that definitely wasn't normal.

His jaw, already loose, dangled slightly to one side.

And worst of all?

He sniffed the air

Mark took several steps back. "Nope. Nope, nope, NOPE."

He whipped out his radio.

"Tom, get here NOW."

Static.

Then—

"I AM LITERALLY IN THE MIDDLE OF SOME-THING."

Mark, backpedaling as Henry started crawling toward him, shouted into the radio:

"Yeah, well, Henry is trying to eat me!!!."

Silence.

Then—

"FUCKING HELL"

Back in town, Tom was gripping the steering wheel so hard his knuckles turned white.

Kevin, still humming in the backseat, suddenly let out a low chuckle.

Tom glanced in the rearview mirror, jaw clenched. "What's funny?"

Kevin, staring out the window with half-lidded, unfocused eyes, made a series of garbled noises that might've been words.

Carl, who had the unfortunate duty of sitting next to zombie Kevin in the backseat, stiffened.

"Boss," Carl muttered, not taking his eyes off Kevin, "I don't think he's—uh—*all there* anymore."

Tom grunted. "No shit."

Carl shifted uncomfortably. "I mean like... *less there* than before."

Tom glanced at Kevin's reflection again.

His posture had slumped even more, and his nose looked dangerously close to falling off.

Kevin, unaware of their conversation, suddenly perked up.

His rotting lips curled into a grotesque approximation of a grin.

He made a wet clicking sound, lifted both hands—

And, for the third time in 24 hours, gave the goddamn finger guns.

Carl flinched so hard his elbow smacked the door. "JESUS CHRIST, KEVIN."

Tom slammed on the brakes.

The patrol car skidded to a stop in front of the jail, and before Kevin could finger-gun them again, Tom threw the door open, stomped around the car, and yanked him out.

"Kevin," Tom said through gritted teeth, "If you try to finger-gun me again, I *swear to God*—"

Kevin, still grinning, immediately did it.

Carl, standing on the other side of the car, whispered, "Holy shit, he has a death wish."

Tom, officially done, dragged Kevin toward the jail by the collar of his Hawaiian shirt.

"Carl," Tom barked, "Go get Mark before Henry actually eats him."

Carl, blinking, hesitated. "Wait, you mean *actually* eats him? Like—"

"CARL. NOW."

Carl scrambled into the patrol car and sped off.

Tom, exhaling sharply, pulled Kevin through the doors of the station, ignoring the confused look from the receptionist.

"Putting him in the holding cell," Tom muttered.

Kevin tilted his head, blinked slowly, and made a confused gurgle.

Tom shoved him into the empty cell, locked it, and walked away without another word.

Kevin, completely unfazed, flopped onto the bench.

After a beat, he let out a soft, wet sigh—

Then raised a single, rotting hand.

And finger-gunned himself in the reflection of the security glass.

Tom saw it.

And nearly flipped the entire goddamn desk over.

Carl had raced out to the woods, expecting to find Mark in a standoff with Henry.

What he found instead was Henry crawling through the grass like an alligator, Mark up a tree, and both of them screaming.

"Mark," Carl shouted, skidding to a stop. "What the hell are you doing?"

Mark, clinging to a branch like his life depended on it, shouted back:

"Holding myself to a higher standard."

Carl **stared.**

Then looked at Henry, who had paused his pursuit long enough to cock his head at him.

Henry's jaw unhinged slightly, and his lips peeled back in a grotesque grin.

Carl immediately regretted his life choices.

"*Okay*, Mark, how do you want to do this?"

Mark, looking down from the tree, shrugged. "Hit him with the car."

Carl's eyes widened. "*What*—?"

"Hit. Him. With. The. Damn. Car."

Henry, hearing this, groaned in protest.

Carl sighed. "Fine. But if Tom yells at me for vehicular assault, I'm blaming you."

Mark gave a thumbs-up from the tree.

Carl, resigned to his fate, threw the car in reverse, then floored it straight at Henry.

There was a thump—

A wet splat—

And then silence.

Henry was now pinned under the patrol car.

Mark climbed down, dusted himself off, and patted the hood.

"Nice work."

Carl, deadpan, muttered, "We are absolutely going to hell."

Tom stood in his office, staring at nothing, debating whether he should quit his job, burn down the jail, or just start drinking.

Then the front door slammed open.

Carl and Mark dragged Henry Voss in, still twitching, covered in dirt, and absolutely pissed off.

Henry sniffed the air.

Then turned toward Kevin's holding cell.

Kevin, who had been lounging like this was a day spa, suddenly perked up.

And grinned.

Henry grinned back.

Then—finger guns.

Tom threw his hat on the ground and stormed out of the room.

"I am NOT paid enough for this."

CHAPTER 28

The Pritchard House was absolute fucking chaos.

Suitcases were half-packed and abandoned on the floor.

The dining table was a war zone of maps, notebooks, and several very poorly drawn route options scribbled in Sharpie.

A cracked laptop sat open with Google Maps pulled up, though the Wi-Fi was as unreliable as Fred's common sense.

The smell of coffee, gasoline, and frustration lingered in the air.

And in the center of it all, Fred sat cross-legged on the kitchen counter, eating the last powdered donut like he hadn't just dropped a bombshell on their entire plan.

"You lost him?" Emmaline repeated, her voice flat with disbelief, her eye twitching like she was seconds from committing a felony.

Fred licked his powdered fingers and shrugged. "Okay, '*lost*' is a strong word."

Kirsten, who was organizing emergency supplies (vodka, duct tape, sage, more vodka), snapped her head up so fast her ponytail smacked Moira in the face.

"What word would you prefer, Fred?"

Fred scratched his horned head, looking deeply contemplative, as though the concept of responsibility was a foreign language he had no intention of learning.

"*Misplaced.*"

A beat of silence.

Joe, standing by the fridge with a half-empty beer, pinched the bridge of his nose so hard it looked like he was trying to push his own soul out of his forehead.

"You *MISPLACED* him ?"

Fred gave finger guns. "That's the spirit."

Joe took a very slow, very deep breath, then turned to Clay and Jeremy, both of whom were staring at Fred like he had just confessed to burning down a children's hospital.

Jeremy, who had been standing quietly up until now, slammed his duffel bag onto the table so hard the saltshaker fell over.

"Let me get this straight." He stepped right up to Fred, practically nose-to-nose.

"You can teleport between realms, manipulate reality, and do all kinds of other freaky demon shit... but you can't keep track of *ONE GODDAMN ZOMBIE?*"

Fred blinked lazily. "Correct."

Jeremy's hands curled into fists. "Joe, can I hit him?"

Joe exhaled. "Not yet."

Fred grinned smugly. "I'd like to see you try."

Jeremy took a step forward, fully prepared to commit supernatural assault, but Clay grabbed his collar and yanked him back before he could lunge.

Jeremy huffed but stayed put, though his eye twitched in a way that suggested Fred's lifespan (or afterlife-span) was now significantly shorter.

Moira plopped into a chair, kicking over a bag of beef jerky in the process. "Okay, so what now?"

Emmaline, who had been the most level-headed up until now, finally cracked.

"We can't leave without Kevin. If we don't bring him to Vegas, Fred could go back on the deal, and then we have an actual rotting corpse problem."

Joe, who had spent the last two weeks regretting every decision that brought him here, muttered, "I hate everything about this."

"Same," Clay agreed, rubbing his temples.

"Double same," Jeremy added, arms crossed.

Fred, still making zero effort to be helpful, grinned through lips now coated in powdered sugar. "Look on the bright side."

Moira snapped her head up. "What bright side?"

Fred licked his fingers clean, shrugged. "At least I didn't misplace both zombies."

A full five seconds of dead silence.

Then:

"*WHAT DO YOU MEAN BOTH ZOMBIES?!*"

Kirsten, who had been aggressively scribbling down a new plan in her notebook, froze mid-sentence.

She looked up very slowly, eyes narrowing.

"Fred."

"Yes, dear?"

"Where. Is. Henry?"

Fred smiled innocently. "That's an excellent question."

"I will stab you."

"Wouldn't be the first time!"

"Fred." Emmaline's voice was low and dangerous, the kind of voice that meant bad things were about to happen. "Where. Is. Henry?"

Fred tilted his head, thinking. "The last time I saw him, he was... um..."

"Fred," Moira warned.

"...wandering toward the train tracks."

Moira slammed both hands onto the table. "*YOU LET A ZOMBIE WALK TOWARD A MOVING TRAIN?*"

"In my defense," Fred said, licking powdered sugar off his lips, "he was already dead."

"*Oh. My. God.*"

Joe slid into a chair and buried his face in his hands. "So now we have to go find Henry too?"

Fred nodded enthusiastically. "Yup! And fast. Before he gets bored and bites someone. Or, you know. Becomes railroad sushi."

Jeremy turned to Joe. "Now can I hit him?"

"Still no," Joe muttered.

"Ugh." Jeremy crossed his arms. "Fine. But if I find Henry eating someone, I get first punch."

Clay snorted but said nothing.

Kirsten, clutching her notebook like it contained the last shreds of her sanity, rubbed her temples.

"Okay, so we split up."

Emmaline nodded, pacing again. "Jeremy, Clay, Joe, you guys head into town and check the usual places. Moira, Kirsten, and I will track Henry toward the tracks, and then we'll meet back here."

"And what am I doing?" Fred asked.

"Staying here and shutting the hell up." Moira said, snapping a piece of beef jerky in half with entirely too much aggression.

Fred put a hand to his chest. "Rude."

Joe stood, sighing, grabbing his keys off the counter. "Alright, let's go before this gets worse."

Jeremy muttered, "How could it possibly get worse?"

Fred, grinning, said:

"Oh, it absolutely can."

Everyone groaned.

CHAPTER 29

Both search teams had come back empty-handed, stomping through the front door like a bunch of pissed-off cryptid hunters who had just spent hours chasing shadows.

Joe, Jeremy, and Clay had been all over town, checking Kevin's old haunts (*Len's Auto Sales, the Gas & Go, the back alley behind Ruby's where he used to "network" with customers*), while Emmaline, Moira, and Kirsten had combed the train tracks looking for Henry.

Nothing.

No footprints.

No trails.

Not a single rotting idiot to be found.

Now, they were all gathered in the kitchen, sweaty, irritable, and ready to throw hands with the universe.

Moira threw herself into a chair, grumbling into her hands. "How the fuck do you lose two zombies?"

"I don't know," Emmaline groaned, leaning against the counter, "but this is getting ridiculous."

Jeremy, who had been leaning against the fridge, cleared his throat. "Uh, about that..."

All eyes snapped to him.

"So, funny story," Joe cut in, grabbing a beer from the counter and popping the cap off with entirely too much aggression. "We didn't exactly find them... but we did find out where they are."

"And?" Kirsten prompted, arms crossed.

Joe took a long sip, sighed, then dropped the bombshell.

"They're in city jail."

The room exploded.

"WHAT?!" Moira shot up from her chair so fast she knocked over a saltshaker. "HOW?!"

"WHY?!" Kirsten added.

"HOW?!" Moira repeated, because she wasn't over it yet.

Joe muttered, "I dunno. Maybe because they're god-damn zombies wandering around town?"

"Okay, valid," Emmaline admitted, hands on her hips, "but also WHAT THE FUCK?!"

"Did they... say anything?" Clay asked hesitantly.

Jeremy snorted. "Dude, they can't talk. They just groan and stare at people."

"Like drunk raccoons," Clay muttered.

Kirsten groaned, dropping her head into her hands. "This is such a fucking mess."

Meanwhile, inside the Albany City Jail, Kevin and Henry were having very different experiences.

Kevin, still wearing the obnoxious Hawaiian shirt, was leaning against the cell bars like he owned the place, lazily swaying in his half-rotten glory.

Henry, on the other hand, looked utterly fucking miserable, sitting in the farthest corner like a man who deeply regretted every choice he had ever made.

Neither of them spoke, obviously.

They just... groaned.

And occasionally stared at things.

Kevin's favorite pastime so far was finger-gunning at the officers every time they walked by.

Henry's favorite pastime was mentally plotting Kevin's demise.

Unfortunately, they were already dead, so neither plan was going very well.

Sheriff Dawson was absolutely fucking over it.

"Alright," he said, dropping his notepad onto his desk, "somebody tell me what the hell we're supposed to do with these two?"

Mark, nursing a cup of coffee that had long since gone cold, squinted at the security monitor.

The black-and-white screen showed Kevin staring blankly into the camera, mouth slightly open, giving a slow, unsettling blink.

Mark shuddered. "Jesus, that one's creepy."

"I don't even think they blink at the same time," one of the deputies muttered. "It's like… one eye goes first, then the other catches up."

Dawson, dragging a hand down his face, turned to Mark. "And you still think it's the witches?"

Mark shrugged. "Who else could it be?"

"I dunno," Dawson muttered, watching Kevin give the camera a slow, double-finger gun again. "Maybe it's just... I don't know. Dumb luck?"

Mark snorted. "Dumb luck turned them into walking corpses?"

"Dumber things have happened," Dawson muttered, reaching for the aspirin in his desk drawer.

"Alright," Emmaline said, taking charge like the only responsible adult in the room. "We need to get them out before someone calls the military."

"How?" Moira asked, kicking her feet up on the coffee table. "Bribe the sheriff? Stage a distraction? Bust them out at midnight?"

"Or" Joe cut in, already regretting being part of this conversation, "we could just... talk to the sheriff like normal people."

Moira blinked slowly. "That sounds legal. I don't like it."

"Too bad," Joe said, grabbing his truck keys. "We're doing it anyway."

"Ugh, fine," Moira muttered, grabbing her jacket. "But if this goes sideways, I'm blaming Fred."

"Oh, absolutely," Jeremy agreed.

Somewhere, in the ether, Fred sneezed.

CHAPTER 30

Before the group could even pile into Joe's truck, shit was already hitting the fan.

Fred, in his infinite demonic wisdom, had decided to be helpful.

Which, for Fred, meant summoning a literal storm cloud inside the kitchen and cackling like a lunatic while everyone screamed and dodged mini bolts of lightning.

"Fred, you useless hell- goblin!" Moira shrieked, hurling a toaster at him.

Fred, mid-air, dodging like an anime villain, grinned. "Oh, I'm sorry, did you need less chaos?"

"YES!" Emmaline snapped, waving smoke away from her face. "You were supposed to help us find Kevin, not turn the house into a goddamn haunted amusement ride!"

"Semantics!" Fred cackled, doing an unnecessary flip just to be a dick. "Look, I got bored. You guys are so slow. I already found them, by the way—"

"They're in jail. We know!" Jeremy shouted over the thunder.

Fred grinned wider, perching himself on the kitchen counter. "Oh, good. Then you already know that one of them is currently trying to eat the evidence locker."

Everyone froze.

A collective oh no settled over the group.

Joe took a deep breath. "Fred. What. The. Hell. Did. You. Do?"

Fred looked positively gleeful. "Oh, nothing. I may have just... let Kevin get a teensy bit more hungry."

"Define teensy," Clay muttered.

Fred gave finger guns. "Let's just say your zombie salesman is now in there real motivated to find a meal."

"Oh for fuck's sake," Emmaline groaned. "Get in the truck now!"

Sheriff Dawson had been having a bad night, but now it was a biblical-level disaster.

Because in the five minutes it had taken for him to step out of his office and take a call, Kevin had managed to:

Break into the evidence locker.

Steal a bag of confiscated weed gummies.

Eat half of them despite being a zombie who doesn't need food.

Start gnawing on a Kevlar vest for reasons unknown.

And Henry?

Henry was just watching it all happen from the cell, sitting in the corner with the most exhausted expression a zombie could possibly manage.

"What the actual fuck—" Dawson started as he stormed into the holding area, eyes wide with horror.

"Uuuuurrrhh," Henry grunted in what might have been an apology.

Kevin, high as a fucking undead kite, swayed slightly, turned to Dawson—

And finger-gunned him.

Dawson stared. "*No.*"

Kevin did it again.

"Absolutely not," Dawson snapped. "Someone fix this!"

Mark, standing beside him, muttered, "What the hell do you expect me to do? Put him down for a nap?"

Kevin attempted a moonwalk but only succeeded in stepping on his own foot and falling over.

"You know what?" Dawson said, throwing his hands up. "I quit. I don't even care anymore. I'll just let the damn witches deal with it—"

And right on cue, the front doors of the station burst open.

Joe, Jeremy, Clay, Emmaline, Moira, and Kirsten practically stormed in, marching toward the front desk like a bunch of reckless idiots who had no idea what they were walking into.

The receptionist, a young woman who had already dealt with enough weird shit for one lifetime, just stared at them, unimpressed. "No."

"Yes," Joe countered. "We're here for the zombies."

She sighed deeply. "Of course you are."

Sheriff Dawson stepped out from the back, rubbing his temples so hard it looked like he was trying to erase his own headache.

"You've got two minutes to explain why the hell I shouldn't just burn your house down and call it a day," Dawson said flatly.

Moira pursed her lips. "Well, that seems extreme."

"Does it?" Dawson snapped, pointing toward the holding cells. "One of them is high. The other one is a glorified corpse lamp post. Neither of them should exist. And I have half a town ready to riot outside because they think it's the apocalypse!"

A brief silence.

Then Kirsten, very helpfully, muttered, "Well, when you put it that way."

"Just get them out " Dawson growled. "Now!"

"Gladly," Joe muttered, marching toward the back.

By the time they got to the holding cells, Kevin had somehow managed to wrap himself in crime scene tape like a bathrobe.

Henry was still sulking in the corner, clearly regretting being undead.

Moira pinched the bridge of her nose. "This is a nightmare."

"I've seen worse," Joe muttered.

"When?!" Emmaline snapped.

"...You don't wanna know."

Clay sighed, reaching for the keys Dawson had begrudgingly handed over. "Alright, let's get these two out before—"

And then Fred materialized out of nowhere.

Right inside the cell.

Kevin perked up immediately, grinning like he'd just found a free buffet. "Ffffffrrrrddddd," he groaned happily.

"Hey, champ," Fred greeted. "You're lookin' good for a dead guy."

Kevin, absolutely thrilled, lifted a hand for a high-five.

Fred, being an absolute gremlin of a demon, actually slapped his palm against Kevin's rotting one like this was a totally normal thing to do.

Moira, watching this, muttered, "I hate everything about this situation."

Fred grinned. "Alright, folks, you got your boys. Let's hit the road before Dawson changes his mind and tries to exorcise someone."

"Why do I feel like we just made a bad deal with the devil?" Jeremy muttered.

"Because we absolutely did," Clay sighed.

Joe, tired of the nonsense, grabbed Kevin by the back of his disgusting Hawaiian shirt and shoved him toward the exit. "Move it, walking lawsuit."

And with Henry shuffling behind them, Kevin high as a zombie kite, and Fred looking entirely too pleased with himself, they escaped the station before Dawson could change his mind.

CHAPTER 31

Sheriff Dawson had officially reached his breaking point.

Albany was a small town. A quiet town. A town where the biggest problem he usually had to deal with was someone's cow getting loose and blocking Main Street for two hours.

But this past week?

This past week had been a shitstorm wrapped in a nightmare, gift-wrapped in absolute lunacy.

And now—

Now he had two zombies, a demon asshole running around, and a town full of people ready to riot.

This was not what he signed up for when he became sheriff.

At exactly 7:12 a.m., Ruby's Diner was already packed, buzzing with conversation, every table occupied.

The second Henry's body had turned back up—and walking this time—people had lost their goddamn minds.

Now?

Now it was the only thing anyone was talking about.

At the counter, old man Everett Jones—who had lived through more Albany bullshit than anyone else—took a long sip of his black coffee and muttered, "This town's goin' straight to hell."

Across from him, Earl Simmons, Albany's self-appointed "expert on weird shit," nodded. "Been sayin' it for years. First, that Pritchard place started actin' up again. Now we got the dead walkin' the streets."

"Ain't natural," chimed in Nancy Wilcox, a lifelong Albany resident who had a habit of clutching her rosary any time something mildly unsettling happened. "It's them girls. Witches, I tell you."

"I heard they been sacrificin' people up there," said Wade Dawson, one of the sheriff's distant cousins, lowering his voice. "Henry was up there snoopin' before he went missin', and look what happened to him."

"Mmmhmm," muttered Marge Talbot, who worked at the post office and knew everything about everyone. "And what about that Kevin fella? He's one of 'em now too. Saw him at the damn car lot the other night, wanderin' 'round like he was still tryin' to sell sedans."

"You ask me," Earl continued, "we oughta do somethin' before this gets worse. People need to take action."

"What you suggestin', Earl?" Ruby asked, raising a skeptical eyebrow as she refilled his coffee.

Earl leaned forward, dropping his voice. "If the law ain't gonna handle it, maybe we oughta handle it ourselves."

Nancy nodded solemnly, clutching her rosary tighter.

"Damn right," Everett muttered. "Back in my day, we knew how to deal with unnatural shit. And we didn't wait for no sheriff to tell us what to do."

Across the diner, Mark—who had just walked in, looking like he hadn't slept in two days—froze mid-step.

Because this?

This was how mob shit started.

"Oh, hell no," he muttered under his breath, turning right back around and marching straight out the door.

Mark slammed the door open so hard Dawson nearly spilled his coffee.

"Boss," Mark panted, leaning against the doorframe like he'd just run a marathon. "We got a problem."

Dawson, who already knew he had about twelve problems, glared up from his desk. "Which one?"

"The town," Mark said grimly, running a hand through his hair. "They're stirrin' up some real bad ideas at Ruby's. Talkin' 'bout takin' matters into their own hands."

Dawson closed his eyes and exhaled. "Goddammit."

"It's bad, boss," Mark continued. "They're convinced the girls at the Pritchard place are behind all this. And they're pissed."

Dawson leaned back in his chair, his jaw tightening.

This town...

This goddamn town.

"Alright," Dawson said finally. "We gotta get ahead of this before someone does something stupid."

Mark gave him a look. "Boss, I hate to break it to you, but we're way past stupid at this point."

"Then we gotta move fast," Dawson said, grabbing his hat and standing up. "Get a couple of guys and meet me at the Pritchard place. If this town's gearing up for some kind of lynch mob, I'd rather not be dealing with another goddamn crime scene tonight."

Mark nodded sharply and hurried out the door.

Dawson downed the rest of his coffee in one gulp, grabbed his badge, and muttered under his breath—

"I shoulda retired last year."

CHAPTER 32

The Pritchard House was a war zone of absolute nonsense.

Between the zombies stumbling around, Fred being an absolute menace, and everyone scrambling to prepare for the ritual, the place looked one minor inconvenience away from burning itself down.

"Alright," Emmaline declared, rubbing her temples like a woman barely holding onto her last shred of patience, "we need to be organized about this. If we don't have everything for the ritual, it's going to be a disaster."

"Bigger disaster than Kevin eating weed gummies and almost getting himself shot?" Moira asked dryly, folding her arms.

"Yes," Kirsten muttered, stuffing a bundle of herbs into a bag. "Because if we screw this up, Fred is going to make our lives hell."

"Oh, I am absolutely going to make your lives hell," Fred cut in cheerfully, floating mid-air like a smug little bastard. "That's a guarantee."

Moira shot him an unimpressed look. "Fred, shut up and make yourself useful."

Fred grinned, snapping his fingers—

And immediately set one of the suitcases on fire.

"FRED!" Emmaline shrieked.

"Whoops," Fred said, sounding exactly not sorry. "Let me try again—"

"Do not try again!," Jeremy cut in, grabbing the suitcase and stomping the flames out.

Fred pouted dramatically. "Ugh, fine. But only because I like you guys. Well, some of you."

"I don't trust that," Clay muttered, packing candles into a bag with suspicious speed.

Meanwhile, Kevin and Henry were not helping.

Kevin, still wearing his crime scene tape sash from the jail, was swaying in place, staring at a lamp like he was trying to figure out how it worked.

Henry, sitting on the couch with an expression of deep existential dread, groaned in pure, silent suffering.

"For fuck's sake," Moira muttered. "Why do we even bother with them?"

"Because they're technically our problem," Emmaline said, shoving a box of chalk into a duffel bag. "And if we don't keep an eye on them, someone is going to shoot them."

"...Fair," Moira admitted.

"Speaking of," Joe said, throwing a couple of supplies into a crate, "we gotta move fast. There's some real bad talk happening at Ruby's. The town's gearing up for something, and I don't wanna be here when they figure out we're all in the same place."

That got everyone moving.

Jeremy was loading crates into Joe's truck while Kirsten double-checked the ritual bag.

Clay, being Clay, was trying to make sure Moira didn't get distracted by Fred's antics.

Which, of course, was not working at all.

"Moira, can you please—"

"Hold on," Moira said, watching Fred as he casually levitated one of the zombies. "What the hell are you doing?"

"Testing a theory," Fred replied, grinning manically. "I was just wondering what would happen if I dropped Kevin from twenty feet up."

"FRED, NO—"

Too late.

Kevin, who had been slowly groaning in confusion, suddenly plummeted from mid-air and crashed through an old table with a sound that could only be described as "bone meets wood meets someone's insurance premium skyrocketing."

There was a long, painful pause.

Then Kevin, from the wreckage, slowly lifted one rotting hand...

And gave finger guns.

Clay sighed aggressively in frustration

"Alright," Emmaline said, hoisting a heavy bag over her shoulder, "we've got everything we need. Let's get moving before Fred decides to start juggling skulls or something."

"Oh, now that you mention it—" Fred started, but Emmaline shot him a glare so lethal that even he shut up.

Joe clapped his hands together. "Right. We pack up, we move out, and we do this ritual properly. Any questions?"

Kevin raised a hand.

"Kevin, No one Cares," Moira snapped.

Kevin lowered his hand, looking mildly disappointed.

Henry, still sulking, groaned in what sounded vaguely like agreement.

"Alright, folks," Joe muttered, glancing at the growing darkness outside. "Let's get this over with before the town gets any bright ideas."

CHAPTER 33

T he Pritchard House attic had seen some shit, but tonight?

Tonight was absolute chaos.

Between two zombies staring blankly at a wall, Fred being an insufferable menace, and half the group barely holding onto their sanity, this was shaping up to be the worst ritual attempt yet.

"Alright," Emmaline declared, like a woman barely holding onto her last shred of patience, "we need to be precise this time. We cannot afford another mistake."

"You mean like the last four times?" Moira asked dryly, folding her arms.

"Or like the time we tried to summon a spirit guide and accidentally called forth a demonic goose?" Kirsten added.

"That was one time," Emmaline snapped. "And technically, that was your fault for mispronouncing the incantation."

"How was I supposed to know the Latin word for 'guide' was so close to the word for 'winged hell spawn'?" Kirsten shot back.

"Guys," Clay interrupted, adjusting a candle, "can we focus? We already have two zombies in the room. If we don't fix this, we'll have a bigger problem than just Kevin and Henry."

Kevin, who had been staring vacantly at a moth circling one of the candles, suddenly let out a wet, gurgling noise.

Henry, sitting slumped in a chair like he'd given up on existence altogether, groaned miserably.

"I think they agree," Jeremy muttered.

"Right, right," Moira sighed. "Let's just get this over with."

Fred, floating smugly above the scene like a demonic theater critic, smirked. "Alright, ladies and gentlemen, let's see if you can manage to do this without completely fucking it up this time."

"We are perfectly capable of pulling off a ritual," Emmaline snapped.

Fred grinned. "That's adorable," he said. "Remind me again how you got Dumb and Dumber over here turned into zombies?"

Kevin, who had been trying to lick the candle flame, made a low, dumb noise in response.

"Shut up, Fred," Moira muttered, tossing a bundle of herbs into a brass bowl and lighting them on fire. "Let's just do this."

Emmaline took a deep breath, raised her hands, and began chanting.

The attic dimmed, the air grew heavier, and an uneasy stillness settled over the space.

For a moment, it actually looked like—

BOOM.

A sudden explosion of sulfurous smoke filled the attic.

"Shit!" Jeremy coughed violently, waving the smoke out of his face.

"That's... definitely more fire than last time," Moira wheezed.

Kevin let out a startled moan, toppled sideways, and landed on Henry.

Henry, already dead inside and out, barely reacted.

The circle crackled violently, glowing an ominous, blood-red hue.

And then—

The smoke began to take shape.

A towering, shadowy figure emerged, horns curling like jagged branches, its eyes glowing like embers. The air vibrated with power. The scent of burning brimstone and bad decisions filled the attic.

And then, in a voice so deep it rattled the floorboards, it spoke—

"Who dares summon—"

"Oh, for fuck's sake."

The demon's booming voice immediately dropped in volume, the imposing figure slumping like an exhausted office worker on a Monday morning.

"Are you fucking kidding me?"

"Fred?" Emmaline blinked, stunned. "Wait, that's you?"

"Yes, it's me," Fred groaned dramatically, rubbing his temples. "I told you idiots, if you don't do this shit right, you just end up summoning me again."

"Goddammit," Moira muttered, kicking over an empty salt container. "We're never gonna get this right."

Kevin, having recovered from his fall, let out a low, pleased-sounding moan and gave Fred finger guns.

Fred finger-gunned him back. "At least he appreciates me."

"At least we know he shows up every time," Kirsten sighed.

"You really wasted a full moon on me?" Fred asked, looking genuinely offended. "This is so embarrassing for you."

"Not as embarrassing as the fact that we're stuck with you," Jeremy muttered.

"Hey, it's not my fault you people are terrible at this," Fred shrugged, hovering slightly above the circle like a smug little shit he is. "You keep trying to summon someone else, and yet—"

He gestured to himself.

"—here I am."

"Well, how do we get rid of you?" Joe asked bluntly.

Fred grinned. "Oh, you don't. Not this time."

"What the hell does that mean?" Clay narrowed his eyes.

"It means I'm sticking around. Permanently," Fred said, cracking his knuckles. "Congratulations, morons. You didn't just summon me—you bound me here."

A horrified silence fell over the attic.

"What the fuck do you mean we bound you here?" Emmaline snapped.

"Oh, it's real simple, sweetheart" Fred said cheerfully. "You messed up the wording in the ritual. Again."

"I am going to scream," Moira deadpanned.

Fred grinned wider. "Go ahead. It won't fix anything."

"We are so screwed," Kirsten muttered.

Kevin, oblivious to the growing panic, let out a slow, delighted moan and patted Henry on the shoulder.

Henry groaned miserably.

"More importantly," Fred continued, stretching his arms above his head, "you still haven't figured out what to do with the zombies. And you should probably do that before the town figures out where they are."

A long, miserable pause.

Then Joe, exhaling sharply, muttered: "Fucking hell."

Fred, grinning like he lived for chaos, finger-gunned the group. "Shall we?"

CHAPTER 34

The attic reeked of bad decisions and burnt herbs. The summoning had failed—again—but now the group had a much bigger problem.

Fred, looking insufferably pleased with himself, was here to stay.

Kevin, blissfully unaware of his own undead predicament, was getting way too comfortable.

And Henry... well, Henry just looked miserable.

"Alright," Emmaline said, rubbing her forehead like a woman who had given up on ever having a normal life. "We need a plan."

"Yeah," Moira muttered. "Because clearly, winging it has worked out so well for us."

Fred grinned, leaning against the air like it was a solid object. "I love that you guys keep trying, though. It's like watching raccoons solve a Rubik's cube."

Kevin, still wearing his Hawaiian shirt, let out a slow, thoughtful moan.

Kirsten narrowed her eyes at him. "What?"

Kevin paused, his rotting brain churning, and then slowly lifted both hands.

Finger guns.

"Jesus Christ," Joe muttered. "Even as a zombie, he's still... Kevin."

Kevin, pleased with himself, groaned happily and tried to high-five Henry.

Henry, dead inside in every sense, let out a long-suffering sigh.

"So," Clay leaned against the wall, staring at the two zombies, "what's the plan? Because keeping them locked in the attic forever probably ain't it."

"Yeah," Jeremy added. "No offense, but Henry's starting to smell worse."

"Hey," Fred interrupted, pointing at Kevin and Henry. "These two are my best work yet! You can't just toss 'em aside like some half-baked experiment."

"Fred," Emmaline sighed, "we are literally trying to avoid a zombie apocalypse here."

"It's one zombie apocalypse," Fred scoffed. "You act like this is a big deal."

Kirsten gestured to Henry's half-detached jaw. "It kind of is, Fred."

Fred rolled his eyes. "Ugh, mortals are so dramatic."

"Okay," Moira said, thinking out loud. "We need a way to keep them contained so they don't wander off and start munching on unsuspecting locals."

"And we need to do it before someone shows up and realizes we have two undead dudes hanging around," Joe pointed out.

"Right," Emmaline muttered. "So what's our best option?"

"We could chain them in the attic?" Kirsten suggested.

"Uh, yeah, that's how horror movies start," Jeremy said. "Next thing you know, one of them gets loose and takes a bite out of the pizza delivery guy."

Kevin, perking up at the word pizza, let out an excited moan.

"No," Clay cut in, ignoring Kevin, "we need something that keeps them out of sight but doesn't make us look like lunatics if someone finds them."

Moira snapped her fingers. "What about the garage?"

"We're not locking them in the garage," Emmaline frowned. "That's inhumane."

"They're zombies," Moira shot back. "And besides, what else are we gonna do? Set up a zombie Airbnb?"

Fred perked up. "Ooooh. I like that idea."

"Fred, no," Kirsten sighed.

"Fred, yes," Fred countered. "The tagline could be 'A killer stay in historic Albany!' Ha! I kill me!"

"Not soon enough," Joe muttered under his breath.

The plan—if one could call it that—was simple:

Escort Kevin and Henry downstairs without them breaking anything.

Sneak them into the garage without any nosy neighbors seeing.

Figure out how the hell to keep them there.

Easy, right?

Wrong.

Kevin, who had spent most of his zombified existence wandering aimlessly, was not built for stealth.

Henry, who was at least more self-aware, seemed mildly horrified by the entire situation.

And Fred?

Fred was being as unhelpful as possible.

"Alright," Emmaline whispered, "everyone stay quiet and move quickly."

Kevin, immediately knocking over a side table, groaned in protest.

Henry facepalmed, which was impressive given that half his face was already falling apart.

"Oh my God," Moira muttered. "If we survive this, I am putting salt around my entire bedroom so Fred can't get in."

"RUDE," Fred gasped, mock clutching his chest. "I am a delight to be around!"

Kevin, losing interest in sneaking, let out a loud, guttural groan.

"NO," Emmaline snapped. "We are NOT moaning dramatically right now!"

Kevin looked personally offended.

Henry, grumbling in his throat, grabbed Kevin by the arm and dragged him toward the stairs.

After what felt like an eternity of pure suffering, they finally got Kevin and Henry into the garage.

Jeremy slammed the door shut, letting out a long breath of relief.

"Okay," Emmaline said, brushing dust off her hands. "That could've gone worse."

"Yeah," Clay muttered. "We could've died."

"Or Kevin could've eaten one of us," Kirsten added.

Kevin, still vaguely listening, gave finger guns.

"Stop that," Moira snapped.

"Okay," Joe exhaled. "Zombies contained. Ritual failed. Fred is now a permanent problem. What's next?"

Everyone turned to Fred.

Fred smiled.

"Now?" he said gleefully. "We wait for the town to figure out they're missing and THEN see how bad things can really get."

Everyone groaned.

"I hate him so much," Jeremy muttered.

Fred just winked. "You're welcome."

CHAPTER 35

Albany was many things—gossipy, judgmental, suspicious of anything remotely different—but it had never been the kind of town that actually got out the pitchforks and torches.

Until today.

Today was special.

Because today, the good people of Albany had officially decided that zombies were the work of the devil, the witches at the Pritchard house had conjured them up, and it was their God-given duty to put an end to it.

The town square was an absolute circus.

Someone—probably that idiot Bill Carter—had taken it upon himself to spread the hysteria like butter on a biscuit, and now half the town was gathered outside Ruby's Diner, shouting about demonic plagues and dark magic.

The other half? Sharpening their damn pitchforks.

Sheriff Dawson stood on the steps of the town hall, arms crossed, face hard as stone, trying to stop this from turning into an actual riot.

"Alright, everybody shut the hell up!" he finally bellowed, his voice cutting through the chaos like a gunshot.

The shouting died down, but the tension remained thick enough to choke on.

"Now," Dawson continued, his jaw tight, "let's all take a breath before someone does something stupid."

"We've already let something stupid happen!" shouted Earl Perkins, the local mechanic. "We got goddamn walking corpses in our town!"

"That ain't normal, Sheriff!" someone else called.

"And who's responsible for it, huh?" Martha Jennings—who had never met a piece of gossip she didn't love—pointed a bony finger toward the Pritchard house in the distance. "The witches, that's who!"

There was a murmur of agreement damn, some more shouting, and one particularly overzealous man raised his shotgun into the air like they were about to storm Dracula's castle.

Dawson rolled his eyes so hard he nearly sprained something.

"Jesus Christ," he muttered, rubbing his temples. "Alright, let's clear up some things before y'all embarrass yourselves further."

"Embarrass ourselves?" Bill Carter stepped forward, eyes wild with conspiracy theories. "Sheriff, are you telling me you don't think it's weird that Kevin and Henry came back from the dead? That those girls up at the Pritchard place just so happen to be involved?"

Dawson sighed. "Bill, I think it's weird that you wear socks with sandals, but you don't see me trying to burn you at the stake."

"This is serious!" Martha shrieked. "Those witches put a spell on Henry and Kevin! And if we don't do something, there'll be more!"

"Yeah!" someone else shouted. "What if there's already more and we don't know it?"

Cue more panicked murmuring.

And that was when Len Tully, the local taxidermist and professional crazy bastard, stood up on the bed of his truck holding a goddamn crossbow.

"I say we go up there and handle this ourselves!"

And that was officially Dawson's breaking point.

In one fluid motion, Dawson yanked his revolver from his holster and shot into the air.

The crack of the gun silenced the crowd instantly.

Len, mid-dramatic declaration, immediately ducked down like he thought he was being targeted specifically.

Dawson, absolutely done with everything, slowly holstered his gun, let the silence settle, then said, very calmly:

"Anyone else wanna keep runnin' their mouth, or can we get back to acting like rational human beings?"

No one spoke.

Good.

"Now," Dawson continued, voice dripping with frustration, "we ain't killing nobody today. Kevin and Henry ain't attacking people, they're not spreading some plague, and whatever the hell happened to them is already being handled."

"Handled how?" Earl Perkins demanded.

"I got my men on it," Dawson said, not technically a lie, "and if you fine folks would stop screaming for blood for five goddamn minutes, we might be able to find a solution that doesn't involve burning down a house in the middle of town like a pack of lunatics."

Len opened his mouth—probably to argue—but Dawson immediately turned and pointed at him.

"You shut up, Len. You don't even live in town, you just like chaos."

Len huffed, crossing his arms like a petulant child. "I do like chaos."

"We know," Dawson sighed. "Now, everyone go home. If I catch even one of you marching up to the Pritchard house with so much as a nasty look on your face, I'll personally haul your ass to jail for disturbing the peace."

A few townsfolk grumbled, but no one moved to argue with him.

After a long, painful pause, Dawson added, "And for the love of all that is holy, someone go get Bill Carter a hobby. I am sick of dealing with his bullshit."

"Hey!" Bill snapped. "I keep this town informed!"

"You keep this town paranoid," Ruby muttered. "Now shut up before you make it worse."

Bill huffed, but wisely backed down.

Dawson exhaled sharply, then, just as calmly as before, said:

"Now if y'all will excuse me, I gotta go figure out how to deal with two undead idiots before one of them manages to sign a car lease or something."

And with that, he turned on his heel and left.

Kevin, now wearing Moira's sunglasses and one of Joe's old hoodies, sat in the garage, waving at passing cars through the cracked door like an absolute freak.

Henry, slumped next to him, groaned.

Kevin nudged him.

Finger guns.

Henry let out the most exhausted moan of his undead existence.

Upstairs, the girls and the guys sat around the kitchen table, frantically whispering.

"Alright," Emmaline said. "Dawson's keeping them from storming the house, but this is getting out of control. We need a plan."

"A plan that doesn't involve Fred," Moira added. "Because his plans involve us 'leaning into the chaos,' and I am not comfortable with that."

Fred, lounging in mid-air, flipped through an old spellbook and smirked. "Your loss."

"So," Joe sighed, "what's our next move?"

A long silence.

Then Kirsten, slowly, hesitantly, muttered:

"We might have to fake their deaths... again."

Everyone groaned.

Fred beamed. "Now we're talking."

CHAPTER 36

The good news: The town wasn't actively marching toward the Pritchard house with torches and pitchforks.

The bad news: That could change at any moment.

The worse news: They still had two undead idiots in the garage, a chaos-loving demon who refused to leave, and absolutely no idea what the hell they were doing.

But, you know. Tuesday things.

"Okay," Emmaline said, pinching the bridge of her nose. "We need to get Kevin and Henry back to being regular dead before someone figures out they're still moving."

"Define 'regular dead,'" Moira said, arms crossed. "Because if you're suggesting we go full 'Night of the Living Dead' on them, I'm gonna need a lot more alcohol."

"We can't just kill them!" Kirsten exclaimed.

"Technically, we'd just be killing them again," Joe said, leaning against the table. "So, like... ethically speaking, it's fine."

"Ethically speaking?" Jeremy blinked. "Did we all just forget that Kevin and Henry still have thoughts? I mean, sure, they're sluggish and Kevin's still an idiot, but they know what's happening."

"Yeah, well," Clay sighed, "we don't exactly have a lot of options, do we?"

"There's always the freezer in the garage," Fred chimed in, grinning mischievously from where he floated upside down in mid-air. "Just pop 'em in like leftovers and—"

"Fred," Emmaline snapped. "You're not helping."

"I disagree," Fred said, flipping himself right-side up. "I think my suggestions have a very practical energy to them."

"Your suggestions are literally always the worst," Moira muttered. "We are not freezing them, and we are not—"

"You could always give them a Viking funeral," Fred interrupted, twirling his fingers. "Set 'em on fire. Very poetic. Also, excellent visual aesthetics."

"Fred!" everyone snapped at once.

Fred held up his hands. "Fine, fine. No Vikings. Boring."

The garage was both a crime scene and a comedy sketch.

Kevin had somehow stolen a pair of sunglasses again and was posing against a broken lawnmower like he was in a used car commercial.

Henry, more resigned than ever, was sitting against the wall, emitting the occasional low groan of existential despair.

"Alright," Moira said, hands on her hips. "We need to get them lying down and very still for when we 'find' their bodies. We need this to be convincing."

Kevin, ever the salesman, gave her finger guns.

"STOP THAT," she snapped.

Henry grumbled and flopped onto the floor, half-heartedly playing dead.

Kevin, seeing this, followed suit—but dramatically.

Like, way too dramatically.

He flung himself onto his back, sprawled out like a man in a murder mystery, then let out an exaggerated "Uuuuhhhhhhhhgggggghhhh!"

There was a long silence.

Joe rubbed his temples. "Kevin, you're dead, not starring in a soap opera."

Kevin, undaunted, groaned even louder, lifting one arm and reaching for the sky like he was dying in a tragic Civil War letter-reading scene.

"For the love of God," Clay muttered.

"No one is giving you an Oscar for this," Kirsten said flatly.

Fred, who was absolutely entertained, floated above Kevin and slow-clapped. "This is some top-tier undead acting. I'm very proud of him."

"Fred, please shut the hell up," Jeremy groaned.

Fred beamed. "Make me."

"Okay," Emmaline exhaled. "So once we set up the 'discovery' of their bodies, we move on to the more im-portant problem: Getting Fred out of our damn house."

"Hey now," Fred pouted, floating just out of swatting distance. "You'll miss me when I'm gone."

"Incorrect," Moira said immediately. "I will celebrate when you're gone."

"Hurtful," Fred muttered, placing a hand over his non-beating heart.

"So how do we actually do this?" Clay asked. "We tried sending him back last time, and it didn't exactly stick."

"We follow the damn ritual properly this time," Emmaline said. "That means no distractions, no screw-ups, and NO Kevin wandering off in the middle of it."

Kevin, who had been eyeing the garage door like he was considering a quick getaway, groaned innocently.

"I saw that," Kirsten said.

Kevin shrugged.

"We should bind Fred to something physical first," Moira suggested. "If he's anchored, it'll be easier to send him back."

"And by 'something physical,'" Fred smirked, "do you mean, like, a random object, or—"

"I mean the most humiliating object possible," Moira cut in, narrowing her eyes. "I will bind you to a ceramic garden gnome if that's what it takes."

Fred paused.

Then, slowly, his grin widened. "You wouldn't."

"Try me," Moira shot back.

After another twenty minutes of gathering supplies, lighting candles, and chanting ominous Latin, they had Fred half-contained in a ritual circle.

It was almost working.

Until Fred opened his mouth.

"Hey, quick question," he said, grinning like the absolute menace he was. "Did you guys double-check the spell this time, or are we gonna summon, like, another surprise guest?"

Everyone froze.

"Fred," Emmaline said slowly, "did you mess with the spell?"

Fred gasped dramatically. "I am offended that you would even suggest—"

Before he could finish, the circle flickered, the air shifted, and the room got noticeably colder.

And then—

The candles flared up, the floorboards creaked ominously, and suddenly—a very loud, very angry voice
filled the attic:

"Who the hell summoned me?!"

Everyone turned to Fred.

Fred grinned.

"*Oops.*"

CHAPTER 37

The moment the voice boomed through the attic, every candle flared like a propane explosion, the ritual circle cracked down the middle, and the distinct scent of burnt toast and brimstone filled the air.

Which, for the record? Not a good sign.

Fred, hovering casually with his arms crossed, looked pleased as hell.

"Oh," he mused, "this is going to be fun."

Moira threw up her hands. "Goddammit, Fred!"

"You all act like this is my fault," Fred said, grinning like a man who had just committed arson for sport. "Technically, you did this."

"Technically," Emmaline snapped, "you tampered with the damn spell!"

"Allegedly," Fred corrected.

"I am going to throw you into the sun," Moira growled.

"You'll have to catch me first," Fred winked.

But before they could strangle Fred into oblivion, the air in the attic twisted, like heat waves rising off pavement. The shadows stretched unnaturally, and the room dropped at least twenty degrees.

Then—

With a horrifying, bone-deep rumble, something stepped out of the swirling darkness.

And by something?

They meant him.

"Beelzeboob!"

The voice ripped through the attic, shaking the floorboards.

"You absolute, festering *failure!*"

Out of the churning shadows, a towering figure emerged. Dark red skin, blackened horns curling from his skull, and flaming eyes that could burn a hole through the fabric of reality itself.

He looked furious.

He looked powerful.

He looked like a demon that had been ripped straight from a medieval nightmare.

Fred, unfazed, tilted his head.

"Oh, shit," he said. "Dad's here."

There was a beat of silence.

Then the entire room exploded into chaos.

"*Who the hell is that?!*" Kirsten yelled.

"*Who do you think ?!*" Moira shouted.

"*Fred, explain !*" Emmaline snapped.

"Oh, you know, just a minor inconvenience," Fred said, grinning like this wasn't an immediate disaster. "Everybody, meet Lord Belphagor. Archduke of the Eighth Circle, Ruler of Sloth and Debauchery, and my ever-so-charming superior."

"Your *what* ?!" Joe choked.

Belphagor stepped fully into the attic, radiating pure demonic energy. The air hummed with the weight of his presence, and the candles snuffed out all at once, leaving nothing but his burning gaze to illuminate the room.

"Do you have any idea how much damage you've caused, Beelzeboob?" Belphagor boomed, his voice a symphony of hellfire and rage. "You were supposed to be back weeks *ago!*"

Fred rolled his eyes. "Alright, first of all, stop calling me that."

"I will call you whatever I damn well please, you incompetent waste of infernal energy!"

"Bit dramatic, don't you think?" Fred muttered.

Belphagor's glowing eyes snapped to the witches.

"And you !"

The girls froze.

"You meddling mortals have no idea what you've unleashed!"

"In our defense," Moira said slowly, "we were actually trying to get rid of him."

"Oh I know," Belphagor growled. "And yet here we are."

From the corner of the attic, Kevin and Henry groaned.

They had been very quietly trying to blend in with the furniture, but Belphagor's furious gaze locked onto them almost immediately.

"What in the nine hells is that?"

"Uh," Kirsten said, wincing. "Funny story..."

Kevin, blinking slowly, gave Belphagor finger guns.

Belphagor visibly twitched.

"Did that *creature* just give me finger guns?!"

"Yes," Moira sighed, "and no one knows why."

"I will smite him," Belphagor declared.

"Please do," Clay muttered under his breath.

Kevin, now looking mildly concerned, tilted his head, letting out a confused grunt.

"Look, big guy," Fred sighed, floating lazily above them all. "I know you're upset, but—"

"Upset ?!" Belphagor bellowed. "Upset does not begin to cover it! You have been wreaking havoc in the mortal plain for far too long, Beelzeboob, and it ends tonight!"

"Alright, first of all, lower your voice," Fred said. "Second of all, it's Fred now, thanks."

"*You don't get to pick your name!*"

"And yet, here we are," Fred smirked.

Belphagor looked dangerously close to combusting on the spot.

"*I am taking you back to hell myself!*"

"Gonna be honest, sounds like a lot of effort," Fred muttered. "Can't we just do this later?"

"So," Jeremy muttered, "do we... do something? Or just let them keep arguing?"

"I mean," Joe said, watching Belphagor and Fred go back and forth like a hellish soap opera, "I feel like we should run, but also, this is kinda entertaining."

"Well, we can't just let them fight in our attic," Emmaline sighed. "At some point, they're gonna start throwing fireballs or something."

"Why don't we just—" Moira paused mid-sentence. Everyone turned to her.

She was staring at the ritual circle, deep in thought.

Then, slowly, her lips curled into a mischievous grin.

"Guys," she said, "I think I know how to fix this."

"Moira," Kirsten said immediately, "we don't have time for one of your half-baked ideas—"

"It's not half-baked," Moira interrupted. "It's actually brilliant."

"This is a trap," Joe muttered.

"Oh, absolutely," Clay agreed.

"Just hear me out," Moira said, grinning. "What if... instead of just sending Fred back... we also send Belphagor?"

The room went dead silent.

"You want to banish the Lord of Sloth and Debauchery to Hell using—what, exactly?" Emmaline asked, raising an eyebrow. "A half-burned candle and some wishful thinking?"

"No," Moira said. "We use a spell from the book."

"The book that got us into this mess?" Kirsten deadpanned.

"Yes," Moira said confidently. "But this time, we actually read the damn thing first."

Fred, who had been listening, turned mid-argument and squinted.

"I feel like I should be offended," he mused. "And yet... I am intrigued."

"Of course you are," Emmaline muttered.

Fred and Belphagor were still arguing.

Kevin and Henry were still confused.

And the gang?

They had just decided on the most dangerous, ridiculous, and completely untested spell they could think of.

Because at this point?

What the hell did they have to lose?

CHAPTER 38

The attic of the Pritchard house was on the verge of supernatural implosion.

On one side: Belphagor, the very pissed-off Archduke of Hell, currently radiating enough demonic energy to set the entire house on fire.

On the other side: Fred, formerly known as Beelzeboob, floating lazily mid-air, looking only mildly concerned about his impending doom.

In the middle: The dumbest group of witches and mortals to ever exist, frantically trying to pull a plan out of their collective asses.

"Alright," Emmaline exhaled, flipping open the spellbook with renewed determination. "We're doing this."

"Define 'this,'" Kirsten said warily.

"We're sending them both back to Hell," Moira said. "Preferably in a way that doesn't get us all incinerated in the process."

Fred grinned. "Aw, and just when I was starting to like it here."

"*Shut up, Fred,*" the group said in unison.

Meanwhile, Kevin and Henry, the undead peanut gallery, were still staring at Belphagor like he was a particularly difficult math problem.

Kevin, after a long moment of profound non-thought, raised a decayed hand and gave him finger guns again.

Belphagor physically twitched.

"STOP THAT!" he roared.

Kevin, completely unfazed, did it again.

Henry, sitting on the floor like an exhausted dad who had given up on life, grunted disapprovingly.

"Kevin," Moira snapped, "if you do that one more time, I swear I will re-kill you myself."

Kevin lowered his hands—but pouted like a child being denied candy.

"Look, can we use them for something?" Joe asked, gesturing to the zombies. "Because they're just standing there being... themselves."

"I mean," Clay said thoughtfully, "we could use them as bait."

Everyone turned to stare at him.

"What?" he said. "Kevin's basically indestructible at this point."

Kevin, as if on cue, tripped over a loose floorboard, fell face-first into a chair, and broke it in half.

Then, without missing a beat, he gave the group a thumbs-up from the floor.

"See?" Clay said. "Totally fine."

"Alright, alright," Emmaline sighed, trying to focus. "We need to modify the original summoning spell. We summoned Fred, but clearly we didn't do it right, and now we have—" she gestured vaguely at Belphagor "—that problem too."

"I HEARD THAT," Belphagor boomed.

"Good," Moira snapped. "Maybe next time, knock before you show up uninvited."

"I am a Lord of Hell. I do not Knock."

"Well, maybe you should start," Kirsten muttered.

"We are not having this damn conversation," Emmaline yelled, snapping the book shut. "We're doing the damn spell."

"Okay, okay," Joe said, holding up his hands. "Let's just go over it first, yeah? Last time, we did it wrong. We can't afford another screw-up."

"Right," Jeremy nodded. "Because when we screw up, things tend to get... worse."

Everyone glanced at Kevin.

Kevin, who had gotten his head stuck in the broken chair, slowly raised one hand and waved.

"...Okay, point taken," Emmaline muttered.

They lit the candles.

They drew the sigils.

They set the circle.

The room hummed with energy, thick and electric, like the air before a thunderstorm.

"Alright," Emmaline exhaled. "Let's send these assholes back to Hell."

"Excuse you," Fred said. "I'm delightful."

"Fred, if you don't shut up," Moira snapped, "I am going to bind you to a decorative plate and sell you at a garage sale."

Fred blinked. "Kinky."

"OH FOR THE LOVE OF—"

"JUST DO THE SPELL," Joe yelled.

The spell started off fine.

The Latin incantation rolled off their tongues, the circle glowed brighter, and the air became unbearably heavy.

Belphagor let out a furious growl, digging his claws into the wooden floor as his form wavered.

Fred, ever the problem, hovered above them like a smug cat. "Oh noooo," he drawled. "Whatever shall I do?"

"Fred, if you fight this, I will personally haunt you for eternity," Moira threatened.

"Noted," Fred said.

And then—

Everything went horribly, catastrophically wrong.

There was a flash of bright red light—

A gust of wind so strong that every candle blew out at once—

And then—

Silence.

Complete, deafening silence.

Emmaline blinked through the darkness.

"Did..." Kirsten started, cautiously. "Did it work?"

A deep, grumbling sigh came from the other side of the room.

"No," said Belphagor's voice.

"Oh good," Moira sighed. "That means Fred is finally—"

"Wait," Jeremy cut in, brows furrowing. "Why does he sound... weird?"

A sudden, horrifying realization dawned on them.

They slowly turned—

And saw Kevin.

Standing there.

With his usual, smug grin.

But when he spoke...

It was not Kevin's voice.

It was Fred.

In Kevin's body.

"Oh, this is interesting," Fred said, stretching his new human limbs. "I have fingers again! Neat!"

The group stared in abject horror.

Moira dropped the book.

"What did we do?" Clay whispered.

"I think we just put Fred in Kevin's body," Joe muttered.

"Which means..." Kirsten swallowed. "Where's Kevin?"

There was a loud, inhuman groan from the corner of the attic.

Everyone whipped around.

Belphagor's body, still huge and demonic, staggered upright—

And let out a furious, otherworldly growl.

"OH HELL," Moira hissed. "KEVIN IS IN BELPHAGOR'S BODY."

The entire room fell silent.

Then, Kevin—now a seven-foot-tall demon lord with literal hellfire eyes—

Gave them finger guns.

CHAPTER 39

The attic was dead silent.

Which was saying something, considering it currently contained:

One smug demon in the body of a used car salesman

One used car salesman in the body of an enraged hellspawn

Three exhausted witches, one exasperated groundskeeper, and one very confused zombie side-kick

Moira was the first to speak.

"Well," she said, blinking rapidly, "this is bad."

"I'd say it's a creative setback," Fred-Kevin corrected, stretching his arms and cracking his neck. "But look at the bright side! I have fully functional limbs again. And a jaw that doesn't fall off when I yawn. Very exciting."

"Oh, for the love of—" Emmaline started, but then—

A low, guttural growl echoed through the attic.

Slowly, everyone turned to face Kevin—or rather, Demon Kevin.

Seven feet of pure muscle, charred red skin, curling horns, and hellfire eyes.

He looked furious.

And then—

He raised a single, massive hand...

...and gave everyone finger guns.

"*FRED*," Kirsten snapped, "fix this!"

"*Oh, no, no, no,*" Fred-Kevin said cheerfully. "I think this is hilarious."

"Fred, he's going to kill us all," Clay pointed out, helpfully.

"Well, yeah," Fred-Kevin said. "But look how well he's handling the horns! I'd say he's adapting beautifully."

Demon Kevin let out a low, unintelligible snarl, stepping forward ominously.

Joe, not taking any chances, immediately grabbed the heaviest object nearby—a floor lamp—and held it like a baseball bat.

"I feel like this is not an ideal situation," Jeremy said flatly.

"Y'think?!" Moira hissed.

Fred-Kevin sighed dramatically. "Alright, fine. I'll help. Eventually."

"What do you mean, eventually?!" Emmaline snapped.

"Oh, I dunno," Fred-Kevin said smugly, "I just think it's fun to watch you all scramble."

Demon Kevin let out a sound that could only be described as a mix between a rabid grizzly bear and a malfunctioning chainsaw.

His clawed hands flexed.

His massive wings twitched.

And then—

With zero warning—

HE PUNCHED A HOLE THROUGH THE ATTIC WALL.

"*OH SHIT,*" Moira screamed, ducking behind a table.

"*HE CAN'T JUST DO THAT!*" Kirsten yelled.

"*HE CAN AND HE DID!*" Joe hollered back.

Kevin, now standing in a cloud of wood splinters and plaster dust, bared his teeth in a terrifying, sharp-toothed grin.

Then, with an ear-splitting roar, he charged at them.

"*RUN!*" Emmaline shouted, grabbing the spellbook.

The group scattered.

Kevin smashed through a chair.

Clay tripped over a candle.

Jeremy barely dodged a flying chunk of attic debris.

Kevin snarled, swiping a massive clawed hand toward Moira—

Who, out of pure instinct, did the stupidest thing possible.

She pulled a Snickers out of her pocket and THREW IT at him.

It hit him square in the forehead.

There was a beat of pure confusion.

Then Kevin stopped, blinking slowly, as if trying to process what had just happened.

And then—

He ate the damn Snickers.

Everyone stared.

"Did... did that just work?" Jeremy whispered.

"No way," Joe muttered.

"Are you kidding me?" Kirsten hissed. "The Snickers commercial *was right?!*"

"Kevin, buddy," Moira tried cautiously, "you feeling any better?"

Kevin-Demon blinked.

Then, very slowly, he raised his hand—

And gave more finger guns.

"Fred," Emmaline said, glaring at Kevin's very smug, very human body, "fix this. NOW."

Fred-Kevin sighed heavily. "Alright, alright. Killjoys."

"Yes, Fred," Clay gritted out. "We are killjoys because we don't want a giant murder demon rampaging through the house."

Fred snapped his fingers.

Nothing happened.

He snapped them again.

Still nothing.

Fred frowned. "Huh."

"WHAT DO YOU MEAN, 'HUH'?!" Moira screeched.

"I mean," Fred said, "this might take longer than expected."

"Define 'longer,'" Jeremy said warily.

Fred grinned. "Oh, you know... a couple hours. A day. Maybe forever."

Everyone immediately lost their shit.

"FRED, I SWEAR TO GOD—"

"You don't swear to God," Fred-Kevin said, winking. "You curse to Satan."

"FRED, I SWEAR TO SATAN—"

"Okay," Emmaline said, rubbing her temples. "We need a new plan. Immediately."

"I still vote we throw him outside and see if he wanders off," Joe muttered.

"And I still vote that you all need to CALM DOWN," Fred said cheerfully. "This is a delicate situation."

"Fred," Kirsten said dangerously, "if you call this delicate one more time, I will feed you *to* Kevin."

Kevin-Demon, chewing on the remains of a chair, let out a pleased growl.

Fred-Kevin sighed. "Fine. Here's the deal."

He leaned forward, lowering his voice conspiratorially.

"We have two options."

"One: We do another spell to swap them back. BUT, considering how stunningly successful your last attempt was, that could also result in, I don't know, merging them into one hideous being, creating an alternate Kevin that haunts your nightmares, or, worst-case scenario, summoning an even bigger problem."

The group stared in silent horror.

"Option Two," Fred-Kevin continued, "we just... wait it out."

"WAIT IT OUT?!" Moira yelled. "THAT'S NOT A PLAN, FRED!"

"Oh, come on," Fred said. "It's Kevin. How much damage could he possibly—"

A thunderous crash came from the hallway.

Kevin-Demon had broken through the attic door and was now casually rampaging through the house.

The group stared.

Then slowly turned back to Fred.

Fred-Kevin cleared his throat. "...I would like to retract my previous statement."

"Good," Emmaline said, gritting her teeth. "Because we are doing the spell."

"Yeah, yeah," Fred sighed. "Fine. But if this backfires? I get to say I told you so."

"If this backfires," Clay muttered, "we'll all be too dead to care."

Moira sighed, rolling up her sleeves. "Let's get to work."

CHAPTER 40

T he attic was a war zone.

The once-orderly ritual circle was now a smoldering mess of melted candles, overturned furniture, and demonic residue that no amount of sage-burning was going to fix. A table was missing a leg. The walls had deep claw marks. And there was a Kevin-sized hole in the door that had absolutely not been there before.

Moira, standing over the wreckage, put her hands on her hips. "Well," she huffed, "I think it's safe to say that this went better than our usual rituals."

"Define 'better,'" Kirsten muttered, brushing charred bits of spell parchment off her lap.

At the center of the chaos stood three very different, equally disoriented figures:

Kevin Rawlins, former used car salesman, current very confused ex-zombie, standing in his Hawaiian shirt, swaying slightly, and looking like he had just woken up from a three-month bender.

Fred, floating in midair once again in his usual demonic form, his cloak somehow looking more wrinkled than before.

Belphagor, the actual terrifying Archduke of Hell, sitting cross-legged on the floor, looking supremely pissed off.

Kevin, finally processing that he was no longer a horned abomination, blinked.

Then, slowly, he lifted his hands—

And gave finger guns.

Moira let out a long, exhausted sigh. "Oh, thank Satan, he's still an idiot."

"Okay," Emmaline said, clutching the spellbook like it was her last shred of sanity. "Did we do it right? Are we all... back where we belong?"

"Define right," Fred said lazily, floating upside down now, because why not.

"Fred, if you are still in Kevin, I swear I will throw you into a church," Moira threatened.

Fred sighed dramatically. "Fine. Test me."

"Okay," Emmaline said, narrowing her eyes. "What's the worst part of being a demon?"

Fred rolled his eyes. "Obviously, the PR. People hear 'demon' and assume you're all about child sacrifices and brimstone. I prefer fine wine, sarcasm, and ruining the lives of bad reality TV contestants."

Moira nodded slowly. "Yeah, that's definitely him."

"Alright, Belphagor," Kirsten gestured to the large, smoldering demon sitting on the floor. "You back in your body?"

Belphagor let out a deep, guttural sigh and stared at his clawed hands. "Unfortunately, yes."

"Okay, Kevin?" Clay asked carefully, stepping forward. "Do you know who you are?"

Kevin frowned. "...Uh."

The group waited.

Kevin squinted at his hands, as if expecting them to still be monstrous claws.

Then he patted his chest, blinked, and grinned. "Well, damn. I think I got my abs back."

"Yep, that's him," Joe muttered.

Kevin stretched his arms overhead, rolled his neck, and took a deep breath. "Man, that was a hell of a ride. You guys ever get possessed by a demon?"

"No," Moira said flatly. "Can't say that we have."

"Well, you're missing out," Kevin said, grinning like this had been a mildly annoying road trip instead of a full-blown catastrophe. "Everything was, like, red, and I could breathe fire, and I think I almost ate someone?"

"Yes," Kirsten said, rubbing her temples. "That was a bad thing, Kevin."

Kevin paused, as if reconsidering. "Right, right. Not supposed to eat people. Got it."

"You say that like it was optional," Joe muttered.

"Hey, it wasn't all bad!" Kevin said, gesturing wildly. "I had wings! Do you know how many chicks dig wings? Like, if I had more time—"

"KEVIN," the entire group shouted in unison.

Kevin paused, clearly unbothered. "What?"

"No more demon talk," Emmaline said, rubbing her forehead. "Let's just be grateful you're human again."

"Debatable," Fred muttered.

"What's that supposed to mean?!" Kevin squawked.

"I mean, you still technically died first," Fred pointed out, floating lazily beside him. "And then you got reanimated. And then you got possessed. So, I'd say your soul is at least lightly used at this point."

Kevin frowned. "Wait. So does that mean I'm, like… still undead?"

"Oh, we'll find out eventually," Fred said, grinning. "Might take a while. I give it six months before something weird happens."

"That is not reassuring , Fred," Moira snapped.

"Alright, so we got Kevin back, we got Fred back, and we got…" Clay hesitated, looking at Belphagor, who was still sitting on the floor, staring daggers at them all. "…him."

"Yes," Belphagor said slowly, voice dripping with loathing. "You got me back. Congratulations. Now, if you don't mind, I would like to get the hell out of here before I incinerate someone."

"Great idea," Joe agreed quickly. "You should definitely leave. Immediately."

"Absolutely," Jeremy nodded. "Doors that way. Or windows. Whatever works."

Belphagor stood, towering over them. "Oh, I will be leaving," he growled, flexing his claws. "But just so we're clear—" his fiery gaze swept over the room "—I will be back."

"Hard pass," Moira said immediately. "You are not invited."

"It wasn't a request," Belphagor snarled, before vanishing in a swirling vortex of smoke and fire.

A long silence followed.

Then Kevin clapped his hands together. "Well! That was fun."

"You died, Kevin," Emmaline said, deadpan.

"Yeah, but I got better," Kevin shrugged. "Anyway, who's up for celebratory drinks?"

"We are NOT drinking with you, Kevin," Moira snapped.

"Speak for yourself," Joe muttered, already walking toward the kitchen. "I need whiskey."

"And I need a vacation," Emmaline sighed. "Some-where far, far away from all of you."

"Oh, you don't mean that," Fred said, smirking. "You love me."

Emmaline grabbed the nearest book and threw it at him.

Fred, laughing, dodged easily. "Oh, come on! You can't get rid of me that easily."

"Don't tempt me," Emmaline muttered.

CHAPTER 41

The silence in the attic stretched on as everyone collectively processed what had just happened.

Kevin was back in his body.

Fred was back to being his insufferable self.

Belphagor had vanished into the ether with an ominous warning.

And Henry Voss, Albany's resident creep, was still standing in the corner.

Still very much a zombie.

Still very much drooling on himself.

Kevin, finally noticing, pointed at Henry. "Uh. What about him?"

Henry let out a low, wet groan and swayed slightly, one milky eye blinking out of sync with the other.

Emmaline pinched the bridge of her nose. "Goddammit."

"Okay," Kirsten said, clasping her hands together. "So, good news—we got Kevin back. Bad news—Henry is still undead."

"And also drooling on the rug," Joe muttered, nudging Henry's foot with his boot.

"So what do we do?" Jeremy asked, glancing at Henry like he might lunge at any moment. "Do we… put him down?"

"Oh, sure," Fred piped up from where he was now floating upside down, completely unhelpful. "Just go ahead and murder a man in cold blood. That'll go great if the sheriff shows up."

"Fred, shut up," Moira snapped. "You literally just got out of Kevin's body—"

"—which was a fabulous experience, by the way—"

"—so maybe sit this one out," she finished.

Fred sighed dramatically. "Fine. I suppose I could help. But only if you say please."

Everyone glared at him.

"You know what?" Clay deadpanned. "Let's kill Fred instead."

"Okay, let's think rationally," Emmaline said, pacing again. "What are our choices?"

"We could re-kill him," Kirsten suggested.

"Violent," Moira said, nodding approvingly. "I like it."

"Not an option," Joe grunted. "If we start killing zombies, people are gonna ask questions."

"Okay, so... exile?" Jeremy suggested. "Just... dump him in the woods?"

"Dude, he's gonna wander into town eventually," Clay pointed out. "What are we gonna do, staple a 'do not feed' sign to his back?"

"We could try another spell," Kirsten offered.

Everyone collectively groaned.

"Yeah," Kevin snorted, "because that's gone so well for us so far."

"Hey," Emmaline snapped, whirling on him. "these were extreme circumstances."

"And the circumstances now?" Fred grinned. "Still extreme. Just less murdery."

"Not helping, Fred!"

"Has anyone actually talked to him?" Clay asked, gesturing vaguely at Henry. "Maybe there's some... I don't know, part of him left in there?"

Everyone slowly turned to look at Henry, who was still standing there, blank-faced, making faint gurgling noises.

"Yeah, I'm not convinced," Jeremy muttered.

"We should at least try," Emmaline sighed.

She stepped forward cautiously, clearing her throat. "Henry?"

Henry tilted his head slightly, making a wet, sludgy sound that did not inspire confidence.

"Henry, can you understand me?"

Henry blinked.

Then grunted loudly and aggressively faceplanted into the rug.

Kevin winced. "Ooof. That looked like it hurt."

Henry made no attempt to get up.

"He's dead again," Moira declared. "Problem solved!"

Fred snorted. "Oh no, sweetie. He's just taking a little undead nap."

"How is that a thing?" Kirsten shrieked.

"Fine," Emmaline grumbled, rubbing her temples. "We're not killing him. We're not dumping him in the woods. We're not performing another half-assed resurrection. So... what? We just keep him here?"

"Well, you could always dress him up and tell people he's an experimental art installation," Fred suggested.

"Fred, I swear to Satan—"

"Orrrr," Fred continued, "you could just—oh, I don't know—keep him in the garage until you figure it out."

The group paused.

"I hate that this is the best option," Moira muttered.

"Same," Clay sighed.

"Okay, fine," Emmaline relented. "We'll stash him in the garage. But Fred—"

"Yes, my dearest, most wonderful, least murdery human?"

"You are in charge of making sure he doesn't wander off."

Fred blinked. "Excuse me?"

"You heard me," Emmaline said, crossing her arms. "This is your problem now."

"I'm sorry," Fred sputtered, "but when, exactly, did I become a zombie babysitter?"

"About ten seconds ago," Kirsten said.

"We'll pay you in sarcasm and begrudging tolerance," Moira added.

Fred scowled. "You people are absolutely insufferable."

"That's the spirit!" Kevin said cheerfully.

Fred let out a long, suffering sigh. "Fine. But if he eats someone, it's on you."

After a lot of struggling, dragging, and one unfortunate moment where Henry bit a chunk out of a couch cushion, they somehow managed to get him downstairs into the garage.

Fred floated above him, arms crossed, looking distinctly unimpressed. "This is degrading."

"Welcome to our world," Emmaline snapped.

Henry let out a gurgly snore.

"Oh, good," Kirsten muttered. "Our zombie has sleep apnea."

"Well, at least he's not wandering off," Joe sighed. "Yet."

"Give it time," Jeremy muttered.

"Alright," Emmaline said, turning to the group. "We deal with the rest of our problems in the morning. For now, I want sleep."

"And I want booze," Moira said.

"And I want to die again," Fred grumbled.

"I can arrange that," Clay muttered.

Fred beamed. "See? I knew I liked you."

CHAPTER 42

Fred, self-proclaimed Demon of Witty Comebacks and Poor Life Choices, had reached his limit.

He'd put up with a lot over the centuries—human stupidity, rival demons with superiority complexes, awkward summoning rituals gone wrong, and, most recently, spending way too much time inside Kevin's rotting carcass—but this?

This was where he drew the line.

Babysitting a zombie? A mindless, drooling, incoherent meat sack who couldn't even hold a conversation? No, thank you.

"That's it," Fred declared, crossing his arms as he hovered over Henry's slack-jawed, drooling form. "I am not wasting another immortal second playing undead daycare."

"Oh, what's the matter, Fred?" Moira mocked, leaning against the garage wall with a smirk. "I thought you loved quality time with the living impaired."

"Yeah, well, I've met tax accountants more interesting than this guy," Fred grumbled, kicking Henry lightly in the side with a spectral foot. Henry snorted, made a sound that was very close to the noise a dying blender makes, and flopped onto his side.

Kevin leaned down, poking Henry's forehead. "I mean... he's still kinda cute, in a grotesque, rotting, jaw-hanging-at-a-weird-angle kinda way."

Everyone stared at Kevin.

"Shut up, Kevin," Emmaline muttered.

"Alright, fine," Kirsten sighed, "What's your plan, Fred? Because I swear to all things unholy, if you say we should just 'let nature take its course,' I will shove your incorporeal ass into a salt circle for eternity."

"Tch," Fred rolled his eyes. "Please. I'm not that irresponsible."

"Oh really?" Clay deadpanned. "Because last week, you turned a priest's holy water into whiskey for fun."

"He enjoyed it," Fred grinned. "I was doing him a favor."

"Fred!" Moira snapped. "Fix. Henry."

Fred sighed dramatically, snapping his fingers as if this whole thing was a massive inconvenience to him. "Fine. But you all owe me a round of drinks after this."

"You don't even drink!" Jeremy pointed out.

"I like watching you drink," Fred said, smirking. "It's hilarious."

Fred floated over Henry's limp form, eyes glowing faintly, fingers wiggling like a magician about to pull a rabbit out of his hat.

"Alright, Undead McCreepy, let's see if we can make you less… soggy," he muttered, placing both hands over Henry's chest.

The air shimmered faintly, a low hum vibrating through the room. The candles flickered. The shadows shifted unnaturally.

And then—

Henry gasped loudly, jerked upright, and let out a massive, gurgling cough.

"Sweet Satan's ass, what the hell was that?!" Henry spluttered, gripping his chest like he'd been hit by a bus.

The entire room froze.

"Holy shit," Moira whispered. "Did... did that actually work?"

"Uh... guys?" Kevin pointed at Henry. "He's still kinda... y'know... grey."

They all stared at Henry.

Fred squinted. "Huh. Whoops. I may have half-fixed him."

"HALF?" Emmaline yelled. "Wat the hell does that mean?"

"It means," Fred said, floating backward slightly, "that technically, he's alive, but, like... still kinda undead. Think of it as... part-time living."

Henry frowned, examining his hands. "Wait... am I still..." He reached up, felt his own face, then moved his jaw experimentally.

And then, slowly, he looked up at them.

"Am I still hideous?"

A long, awkward silence followed.

Kevin opened his mouth.

Moira kicked him in the shin before he could answer.

"No, Henry," Kirsten lied. "You look... great."

"Fantastic," Joe said, not looking at him.

"Peak physical condition," Jeremy added, grinning too widely.

Henry grinned, his half-rotted lips stretching in a way that made Clay physically recoil. "Hell yeah."

"So what the hell is he now?" Clay asked, still keeping a very safe distance from Henry. "Like, undead but alive?"

"Basically," Fred shrugged. "I reanimated the parts that weren't completely beyond saving. He's still got a little zombie in him, but I'd say he's... 70% human now."

"What about the other 30%?" Moira narrowed her eyes.

Fred grinned deviously. "Oh, I don't know. Guess we'll find out, huh?"

"FRED," Emmaline yelled.

"What?" Fred grinned. "He's not dead anymore. You wanted me to fix him, I fixed him. It's not my fault he's got some lingering side effects."

Henry, completely ignoring the conversation, flexed his arms and admired himself. "Y'know what? I feel great. I could eat a damn horse right now."

Everyone immediately tensed.

Henry blinked. "Uh. Not, like… literally. Just… I'm hungry."

"Right," Joe muttered, side-eyeing him. "Sure."

"Let's just… keep an eye on that," Kirsten said carefully.

Fred snickered. "Oh, don't worry. If he gets too snacky, we can always put him down for a real nap."

Henry glared. "Dude, you literally just brought me back. Give me five damn minutes before you threaten to kill me again."

Fred grinned wider. "No promises."

"Okay," Emmaline sighed. "So. Henry's alive. Kind of. Whatever. Fred, you're done messing with him. No more alterations. We're gonna monitor him and make sure he doesn't start trying to eat anyone."

"Fair," Henry shrugged. "No promises, though."

"Not funny, Henry," Jeremy warned.

"I'm just saying, if a guy happens to be made of steak—"

"HENRY!"

Henry laughed, throwing his hands up. "Alright, alright! I'll behave. Probably."

"This is our life now," Moira groaned, dropping onto the couch. "Zombies, demons, idiots, and impending doom. I need a drink."

"Same," Clay muttered.

"Well, I feel great," Kevin said, stretching. "So what's next?"

"We need to get Fred the hell out of here," Kirsten said, pointing at the smug floating menace. "He's officially overstayed his welcome."

Fred grinned. "Aw, you're gonna miss me when I'm gone."

"Not if we get you out fast enough," Joe muttered.

"Alright, then!" Fred clapped his hands. "Next stop: Getting me the hell outta this dump!"

And, for once, everyone completely agreed.

CHAPTER 43

F red had one rule in life (or whatever state of existence he was in): Never do more work than necessary.

And yet, here he was, floating in the garage, surrounded by idiots, being pressured into actually fixing Henry correctly this time, which was really more work than necessary in his opinion.

He had already partially brought Henry back. Wasn't that enough?

Apparently not.

Because now Henry was stuck in some weird half-human, half-zombie state, which Fred thought was hilarious but no one else seemed to appreciate.

"Oh, come on," Fred whined, hovering dramatically above the group. "You people are so demanding. I already brought the guy back! So what if he's a little dead still?"

"Fred," Emmaline snapped, "fix him. Completely. Before we send your insufferable ass back where you belong."

Fred sighed deeply, running a hand through his incorporeal hair. "Fine, fine. But just so we're clear, I don't want to do this. I resent this. I want my displeasure to be noted and documented for all of demon history."

"Duly noted," Moira deadpanned. "Now shut up and get on with it."

Fred dramatically cracked his knuckles (despite having no actual bones) and hovered over Henry, who was still sitting on the floor looking mostly confused but also vaguely pleased with himself.

"Alright, Henry," Fred said, rolling up his spectral sleeves. "This might tingle. Or it might be excruciating. Who's to say?"

"Wait, what?" Henry blinked. "That doesn't sound—"

Fred clapped his hands together, sending a shock-wave of energy crackling through the air. Candles flickered, the temperature dropped, and Henry immediately seized up like he'd just been electrocuted.

"Holy Sh—" Kevin started, jumping back as Henry convulsed wildly, letting out a sound that could only be described as an old fax machine dying.

"What the hell, Fred?!" Kirsten yelled, shielding her face from the surge of power filling the room.

"He's FINE!" Fred yelled back. "This is just a little dramatic effect!"

"A LITTLE?!" Moira shrieked.

Henry, meanwhile, was levitating. His entire body was glowing, his limbs snapping back into place with a series of wet, unsettling pops.

"*Is this normal*?" Henry screamed, twisting in the air like a possessed marionette.

"Nope!" Fred grinned, snapping his fingers one last time.

With a final Snap, Henry dropped like a sack of potatoes onto the garage floor.

Everyone stared at Henry's motionless body.

"...Did you just kill him again?" Clay asked slowly.

"Hold on," Emmaline said, stepping closer. "Henry? Are you—"

Henry suddenly sucked in a HUGE breath and sat bolt upright.

"AAAAHHHHHHHHHH!!"

"AAAAHHHHHHHHHHH!!" Kevin screamed back out of instinct.

"Stop *SCREAMING!!*" Kirsten yelled.

"I'm Alive!!" Henry shouted, patting himself down frantically. "I can feel my face! Oh My God, I'm Warm! I have a pulse! I—"

Henry suddenly stopped talking.

His expression dropped into something horrified.

His eyes went wide.

"Oh my god."

"What?" Jeremy asked, immediately tense. "What's wrong?"

Henry slowly lifted his hands, turning them over as if he couldn't believe what he was seeing.

"I..." Henry swallowed hard. "I have zombie memories."

The room went dead silent.

Henry looked at Kevin.

Kevin looked at Henry.

And then, at the exact same time, they both shouted:

"OH MY GOD, I ATE A SQUIRREL!!"

Everyone gagged.

"Oh come on," Moira yelled, covering her ears. "Why would you say that out loud?!"

"It was *raw*!!" Henry howled, his face in his hands. "I can still taste it!!"

"Stop talking!!" Emmaline yelled. "Stop talking right now!!"

"Alright, well," Fred sighed, dusting off his hands like he had just finished an honest day's work. "Looks like my job here is done!"

"Wait, wait, wait," Kirsten grabbed his arm before he could disappear. "You're not off the hook yet."

Fred groaned. "What now?"

"We had a deal," Emmaline said firmly. "You fix Henry, and then we send you back where you came from."

Fred grimaced. "Right. That part."

"Time's up, Fred," Moira said sweetly. "Pack your bags. It's time to go."

Fred looked around at the group, pouting like a child who just got told recess was over. "You guys suck, you know that?"

"Yep," Clay nodded. "Bye, Fred."

"Fine!" Fred huffed, floating toward the center of the room. "But don't come crying to me when you get bored without my radiant personality around!"

"We won't," Jeremy said flatly.

"Not even a little bit," Joe added.

Fred rolled his eyes, then clapped his hands together.

The air rippled, shadows danced across the walls, and for a brief moment, the scent of burnt cinnamon filled the garage.

"Later, losers," Fred grinned, throwing up finger guns.

And with a final, dramatic pop, Fred vanished into the ether.

A deep silence settled over the garage.

"Is... is he actually gone?" Moira asked cautiously.

"I think so," Emmaline said, glancing around warily. "No more obnoxious commentary. No more floating smirk. I think we finally did it."

"Thank Satan," Kirsten breathed, collapsing onto a chair. "I was two seconds from exorcising him with my fists."

"Alright," Clay said, rubbing the back of his neck. "So. What now?"

Henry looked down at himself, still in shock that he was fully human again.

Kevin shrugged. "We go back to pretending this town is normal?"

"Too late for that," Joe muttered.

"I don't know about y'all," Moira said, standing up, "but I need a damn drink."

"Same," Kirsten agreed. "And I need to bleach my brain after hearing about the squirrel."

"Never speak of it again," Henry yelled.

"Deal," Emmaline said quickly.

And with that, the group dragged themselves upstairs, exhausted, exasperated, and very much over the events of the past week.

Fred was gone.

Henry was fixed.

Kevin was... well. Kevin.

And tomorrow?

Tomorrow was another problem entirely.

CHAPTER 44

A new day dawned over Albany, but it wasn't peaceful.

It wasn't quiet, either.

Because the town was still out for blood.

The lynch mob hadn't disbanded. If anything, after a night of stewing in their own paranoia, the locals had only become more determined to take action.

They still thought Henry and Kevin were undead monstrosities.

They still believed the witches had something to do with it.

And the sheriff?

Sheriff Dawson was just as clueless as the rest of them.

By sunrise, a crowd had gathered outside Ruby's Diner.

Some of them looked like they hadn't slept at all, their faces pale and drawn from a mix of fear, anger, and caffeine overload. Others looked far too eager, gripping shotguns, makeshift torches, and—bizarrely—a handful of pitchforks.

"Alright, everybody shut the hell up!" Clyde Mason, one of the louder town busybodies, stood on a rickety wooden crate near the curb, arms crossed like a man who had way too much free time and way too little common sense. "Ain't nobody seen hide nor hair of them zombies since last night. And if we don't do somethin' about it, who's to say they ain't hidin' up at the Pritchard place?"

"That's what I've been sayin'!" Vern Tate, the owner of Tate's Hardware, spat into the dirt. "They been up to no good since the second they moved into town. Witches! And now we got demons and the dead walkin'!"

"First Henry goes missin'," someone else muttered. "Then he comes back from the dead? What kinda unnatural shit is that?"

"I heard one of them demons made a deal with the girls up there," Mabel added in a conspiratorial whisper. "Ain't no good gonna come from that house. You mark my words."

"I say we go up there and drag 'em out!" Clyde barked.

A murmur of agreement spread through the crowd.

The mob mentality was taking hold.

Sheriff Dawson arrived just in time to see the first shotgun get cocked.

"Alright, alright!" Dawson bellowed, storming through the crowd like an angry bear who had just been woken up too early. "Everybody calm the hell down before someone does something stupid."

"Too late for that," Deputy Mark muttered beside him, glaring at Clyde and Vern specifically.

Dawson yanked the crate out from under Clyde, sending the man toppling into the dirt with a loud grunt.

"Let's get somethin' straight," the sheriff growled, adjusting his hat as he stared them all down. "I don't give a damn what y'all think happened. What I know is that we don't solve our problems with goddamn torches and pitchforks. We ain't some medieval lynch mob, and this ain't Salem."

"But Sheriff—!" Vern started, but Dawson cut him off with a glare so sharp it could've stripped paint.

"I said shut it, Vern."

The crowd shifted uneasily, but no one dared challenge Dawson outright.

"Now," Dawson continued, "I don't know what's goin' on yet. But I do know Henry Voss and Kevin Rawlins are still both missing—"

"Missing?!" Clyde sat up from the dirt, confused. "I thought you said they were—"

"As far as we know," Dawson interrupted, "they're missin'. Ain't nobody seen 'em since last night and until I get proof otherwise, that's what I'm goin' with."

"Then we should go check that house!" someone called from the back.

"Yeah!" another agreed. "Ain't it suspicious they ain't been down here since last night?"

"You goin' soft on them witches, Dawson?" Vern prodded, a sly smirk on his face. "Or did they put a spell on you too?"

The crowd muttered in agreement, some nodding.

Dawson let out a slow, heavy sigh.

"Mark," he muttered to his deputy. "Go fetch me the biggest bottle of aspirin you can find. I got a headache already."

Kevin Rawlins—fully human again, but still vaguely traumatized by the past few days—was lying face down on the couch in the living room of the Pritchard house, groaning into a throw pillow.

"Why do my bones feel weird?" he mumbled. "Were they always this... bone-y?"

"Yes, Kevin," Kirsten said dryly, flipping through a spellbook. "Your bones have always been made of bones."

"Ugh," Kevin flipped onto his back, staring at the ceiling. "I miss being dead. Less existential dread."

"No, you don't," Emmaline corrected, tossing a book at him. "Now shut up. We've got bigger problems."

"Like the angry mob that still thinks y'all are zombies?" Jeremy guessed, leaning in the doorway with his arms crossed.

"Bingo," Moira sighed, rolling her shoulders. "And let me guess—Dawson's trying to talk them down while failing miserably?"

"That's the general idea," Clay added, pacing by the window. "Town's about ten seconds from turning into a full-blown horror movie pitchfork riot."

"Great," Emmaline muttered. "Love that for us."

"So what do we do?" Kevin asked, sitting up. "I mean, I could go out there and prove I'm alive—"

"That's the stupidest idea I've ever heard," Joe interrupted. "They'll just assume you're a smart zombie."

"I am smart," Kevin argued. "I sold three extended warranties the week before I died."

"I rest my case," Joe said flatly.

"Alright," Emmaline sighed, rubbing her temples. "We need a plan. Because if we don't handle this right, the next thing we summon will be an ambulance."

CHAPTER 45

D awson was done.

So incredibly done.

The town wasn't listening, the crowd was getting louder, and he could already see a few hot-headed locals starting to stir up more trouble.

And then—

A truck screeched to a halt nearby.

Dawson turned.

And out stepped Doc Harris, the town doctor, looking more stressed than ever.

"Sheriff!" Doc called, striding over. "You're gonna wanna hear this."

"If it ain't news about a sudden outbreak of common sense, I don't wanna hear it," Dawson muttered.

"It's about Henry," Doc said gravely. "And Kevin."

The crowd fell silent.

"What about 'em?" Vern asked.

Doc took a deep breath. "I just saw 'em. Alive. And... well. We got a problem."

By the time the first gunshot rang out, the town was already teetering on the edge of complete anarchy.

Sheriff Dawson didn't have time for this.

The mob outside Ruby's Diner was still grumbling and muttering, still clutching their shotguns, pitchforks, and wildly misplaced sense of self-righteousness.

And now, some trigger-happy idiot had decided to escalate things.

"Mark!" Dawson barked at his deputy. "Get in the damn car!"

Mark, who had long accepted his role as the sheriff's unwilling sidekick in this town's ongoing saga of stupidity, did not argue.

The sirens wailed to life, and the police cruiser sped toward the gunfire.

Kevin Rawlins had never been a particularly fast runner.

He was more of a "fast talker, slow thinker" kind of guy.

Which was a problem because right now, he was sprinting for his goddamn life.

"WHY ARE YOU SHOOTING AT ME?!" Kevin screeched over his shoulder, dodging behind a used Nissan Altima.

"BECAUSE YOU'RE SUPPOSED TO BE DEAD, DAMMIT!" Old Man Baxter shouted, reloading his shotgun.

Kevin, panting like a dying mule, threw up his hands. "I AM NOT DEAD!"

"THAT'S EXACTLY WHAT A ZOMBIE WOULD SAY!"

"OH FOR FU—" Kevin grabbed the nearest object—a goddamn hubcap—and launched it at Baxter's head.

Baxter staggered back, clutching his forehead. "YOU LITTLE SHIT!"

Kevin didn't stick around.

He bolted, careening through the parking lot like a man whose day had gone completely off the rails.

And that was exactly when Henry Voss rounded the corner.

Henry had just bought himself a Dr Pepper at the Gas & Go and was about to enjoy his first sip of the day when Kevin—panicked, wild-eyed, and half-running, half-tripping like a giraffe on ice—slammed into him at full speed.

Henry grunted as his soda flew from his hand and hit the pavement.

"HENRY, JESUS CHRIST, WE GOTTA GO!"

"What the hell?!" Henry wheezed, trying to untangle himself from Kevin. "What are you—"

"No time!" Kevin grabbed him by the collar and dragged him into a side alley. "Some old freak is trying to kill me!"

Henry glanced back.

Sure enough, Old Man Baxter was hobbling toward them, shotgun in hand, looking like he was having the time of his goddamn life.

"...Again?" Henry deadpanned.

"Yes, again!"

"I hate this town," Henry groaned.

"Me too!"

"We should've stayed dead."

"Yes!"

They both nodded in mutual agreement.

Then—

A shotgun blast tore through the dumpster next to them.

"Are you serious right now?!" Henry yelled.

"What is *wrong* with this town?!" Kevin shrieked.

They took off running just as Sheriff Dawson's cruiser screeched to a halt at the end of the alley.

"BOTH OF YOU, FREEZE!" Dawson bellowed, door swinging open as he stepped out of the car.

Kevin and Henry skidded to a stop so fast they almost fell over.

"Oh my god," Kevin whispered. "I'm about to get arrested again."

"I literally just wanted a Dr Pepper," Henry muttered. "I didn't even want to be alive today."

"You two are the dumbest sons of bitches in this whole town," Dawson grumbled.

"Technically," Kevin pointed out, "I was the second dumbest before Henry came back."

"Gee, thanks," Henry said flatly.

Before Dawson could decide whether to shoot them both out of principle, a voice hollered behind him.

"Sheriff! Get out the way, I gotta put 'em down!"

Dawson turned.

And saw Old Man Baxter—still holding his damn shotgun—limping toward them like some deranged Wild West bounty hunter.

Dawson snapped.

"Oh for the love of —Put the goddamn gun down, Baxter!"

Baxter scowled. "You don't understand, Sheriff! That one ain't right!" He pointed a gnarled finger at Kevin. "That's a dead man walkin'!"

"No," Dawson said flatly, "that is a very stupid man walkin'."

Kevin crossed his arms. "Rude."

"And that one—" Baxter pointed at Henry. "—he was dead! We all saw it!"

"Yeah, I know," Dawson grumbled. "It's been a weird couple of days. But I can confirm: they're both alive."

"Coulda fooled me," Baxter sniffed.

Dawson rolled his eyes so hard he almost saw the back of his own skull. "Jesus H. Christ, you can check their damn pulses yourself if you want, but you're the one who's going to jail today, Baxter."

Baxter's grin faltered. "Wait, what?"

"Oh yeah." Dawson stepped forward, pulling out his cuffs. "Shooting at civilians? You bet your ass you're going to jail."

"But—but they were dead!"

"Well, they ain't now!"

"This is bullshit!"

"I agree," Kevin muttered, dusting himself off. "But mostly because I was the one getting shot at."

Dawson ignored him. "Mark, take his ass in. I ain't got the patience for this."

Mark grabbed Baxter by the arm and started hauling him toward the car.

"This ain't right!" Baxter howled. "The dead should stay dead!"

"You keep talkin', and you're gonna wish you were dead," Dawson muttered.

Kevin snorted. "Damn, Sheriff. Didn't know you had jokes."

"Shut up, Kevin."

With Baxter cuffed and loaded into the cruiser, Dawson turned back to Kevin and Henry.

"So," Dawson grumbled. "Do either of you morons have an actual plan for how to fix this mess?"

Henry sighed. "Believe it or not, we do."

"And I have nothing to do with it," Kevin added quickly. "I just want that on the record."

Dawson stared at them.

Then took a long, slow breath.

"Go home," he finally said. "Stay there. And for the love of God, don't make this worse."

"Define worse," Kevin muttered.

Dawson pointed at him. "Shut. Up."

And with that, he stormed off to take Baxter to jail.

Henry and Kevin watched him go, then looked at each other.

"You wanna get that Dr Pepper now?" Kevin asked.

Henry groaned. "I wanna get hit by a truck."

"That's fair."

CHAPTER 46

Kevin and Henry had somehow, against all odds, made it back to the Pritchard house in one piece.

Neither of them was entirely sure how.

Kevin was 99% certain it had something to do with his natural charisma, while Henry was 100% certain it had more to do with Sheriff Dawson threatening to pistol-whip anyone who so much as looked at them funny.

Either way, they were alive, they were breathing, and—most importantly—they were no longer being shot at.

That was the good news.

The bad news?

A mob of angry townsfolk was currently marching toward the Pritchard house, torches and pitchforks in hand, looking like a budget version of a Universal monster movie.

"...Shit," Henry muttered, peering out the window.

"Oh, come *on*," Kevin groaned. "I just got back!"

"Well," Emmaline sighed, crossing her arms, "guess it's time to go make some friends."

Sheriff Dawson had barely left town before things had gone completely to hell.

It had started with a few angry whispers at Ruby's Diner.

Then someone said, "Henry and Kevin are witch-raised abominations."

Then Clyde Mason shouted, "They need to be dealt with."

And now—here they were.

Thirty angry citizens stomping up the driveway toward the Pritchard house, weapons in hand, fueled by blind rage and absolutely no common sense.

The usual suspects were at the front:

Clyde Mason, who had somehow become the self-appointed leader.

Vern Tate, who was only here because Clyde owed him money and this   seemed like a good way to pressure him into paying up.

Mabel, who swore she "wasn't racist," but had called the   girls "them witchy types" at least seven times that morning.

Randall Cobb, who honestly just enjoyed a good riot.

And Doc Harris, who should have known better, but was already three   bourbons in.

"Come on out, ladies!" Clyde bellowed, slamming his fist against the porch railing. "We ain't leavin' 'til we get answers!"

"Answers to what?" Kirsten called from the front door, voice dripping with exasperation.

"To what the hell y'all did to Henry and Kevin!" Clyde shot back. "And whatever else you been con-jurin' up in there!"

"That's rich," Moira muttered under her breath. "Like half these idiots haven't spent the last decade selling their souls for deer-hunting luck and better crop yields."

"I KNOW Y'ALL HEARD ME!" Clyde shouted. "I SAID, GET OUT HERE!"

"We heard you fine," Emmaline said, stepping out onto the porch with her arms crossed. "We just don't appreciate being yelled at."

"Or being accused of dark magic when we barely managed to get our last spell to work without accidentally summoning another demonic farm animal," Moira added.

"Which was NOT our fault," Kirsten cut in. "The ritual book was missing a page!"

"STOP TALKIN' IN YOUR DEVIL TONGUE AND FACE US LIKE WOMEN!" Clyde snapped.

"Clyde," Kirsten deadpanned, "we're literally speaking English."

"IT SOUNDS LIKE LIES!"

"Everything sounds like lies when you're that stupid," Moira muttered.

Vern, meanwhile, squinted past them and spotted Kevin and Henry in the window.

"THERE THEY ARE!" he hollered, jabbing a finger toward the house. "SEE?! THEY'RE STILL MOVIN' AROUND!"

"Of course we are, you dumbass!" Kevin snapped, flinging open the front door and stomping onto the porch. "I have a goddamn heartbeat, you can come check if you want, but if you touch me, I will press charges."

"...Kevin, you ain't exactly the most trustworthy source," Doc Harris slurred.

"EXCUSE ME?!" Kevin looked genuinely offended. "I am a businessman, sir! A pillar of this community!"

"You were a used car salesman who faked your own injury for insurance money," Doc pointed out.

Kevin huffed. "Irrelevant!"

"Look," Emmaline said, cutting in before Kevin made things worse, "we get it. Y'all are scared. But I promise you—whatever happened, it's fixed now."

"Bullshit," Clyde growled. "Ain't nothin' fixed 'til we see some proof."

Henry sighed and pushed past the girls onto the porch. "What, you want me to die again to prove a point?"

"WELL—" Clyde hesitated, like he was genuinely considering it.

"OH MY GOD," Moira threw up her hands. "What do you want?! You wanna cut them open and see if they bleed?! You wanna drown them like in the Salem witch trials?! What's the stupidest possible way you'd like us to prove that they're fine?"

"...Can they eat?" Mabel finally asked.

Everyone blinked.

"Excuse me?" Kirsten said flatly.

"Zombies can't eat real food," Mabel said, crossing her arms. "Make 'em eat somethin'."

"...That is the dumbest—"

"Fine!" Kevin shoved past Emmaline, stormed back inside, and emerged two seconds later holding a slightly stale apple fritter from Ruby's Diner. "HERE! YOU WANNA SEE ME EAT?!"

Without breaking eye contact, he took the biggest goddamn bite anyone had ever seen.

Chewed.

Swallowed.

And then, because he was a petty son of a bitch, he licked his fingers and grinned.

"Mmm. Delicious. Want a bite, Clyde?"

Clyde stared at him.

Kevin stared back.

"Well... shit," Clyde muttered.

"Told you," Kirsten muttered.

The mob started shifting uncomfortably.

A few of them scratched their heads.

A few of them awkwardly shuffled their feet.

And then Vern, finally admitting defeat, just sighed and said:

"Guess we look real dumb now, huh?"

"Yup," Doc muttered. "Real dumb."

"So... what now?" Randall Cobb asked.

"Now," Emmaline said, "y'all get off our damn lawn."

Fifteen minutes later, the mob had mostly dispersed, though some townsfolk hung back, still grumbling about magic and witchcraft and the general state of the world.

Kevin plopped down onto the porch steps, still chewing his fritter. "Well, that went well."

"Did it?" Henry muttered.

"Nobody got burned at the stake," Moira pointed out. "That's a win."

"For now," Kirsten said, watching as Clyde and the others trudged back toward town. "But you know how this town is. It ain't over yet."

"Let 'em try," Kevin muttered, leaning back with a smirk. "If anyone comes at me again, I'm biting 'em just to make 'em panic."

"KEVIN!"

"What? I'm joking! ...Mostly."

Emmaline groaned and rubbed her temples. "God help me."

Kevin grinned. "Oh, sweetheart. You have no idea."

CHAPTER 47

By the next morning, Albany had mostly returned to normal—if you could call it that. The townsfolk had slinked back into their daily routines, the sheriff had given up on trying to keep people from doing stupid things, and Kevin had miraculously survived being both sacrificed and undead.

The Pritchard House, still looming over its sprawling, overgrown estate, stood victorious—a little worse for wear, slightly more haunted than before, but still standing.

Inside, the girls, Joe, Jeremy, and Clay sat around the kitchen table, nursing cups of coffee like battle-weary survivors.

The night before had been a lot.

But they had made it.

They were alive.

Kevin was alive.

Henry was alive.

Fred was still a problem, but one thing at a time.

Joe stretched his arms over his head and let out a long sigh. "Well, that was one hell of a mess."

"No kidding," Jeremy muttered, "And we still gotta deal with whatever the hell Fred is up to."

"You don't deal with Fred," Kevin said, looking far too relaxed for someone who had just spent the last few days as a literal corpse. "Fred does whatever Fred wants."

"Well, Fred can take his 'whatever' and shove it," Emmaline muttered, stirring her coffee aggressively. "We've had enough supernatural nonsense to last a damn lifetime."

"Agreed," Kirsten said. "We should lay low for a while. Act normal. Blend in."

"Blend in?" Moira snorted. "We literally just turned an undead Kevin back into a sleazy Kevin. You think this town is gonna forget that anytime soon?"

"Weirder things have happened," Clay pointed out.

Moira raised an eyebrow at him. "Have they, though?"

Clay smirked. "Well, there's this happening right now."

Before Moira could even ask what he meant, he leaned forward and kissed her.

It wasn't some grand cinematic moment—it was soft, confident, and surprisingly natural, like something that had been waiting to happen for a long time.

For once, Moira had nothing smart to say.

She just blinked at him for a moment before muttering, "Huh. Okay then."

"That's it?" Kevin asked, leaning forward eagerly. "No dramatic swooning? No throwing a drink in his face?"

"Oh, shut up, Kevin," Moira said, kissing Clay again just to make a point.

Kevin, visibly horrified, groaned and covered his face. "Oh God, I take it back. Stop. Too much romance. I need bleach for my brain."

Joe, watching the whole thing with amusement, shook his head. "Well, hell. If that don't beat all."

"Y'all could've just told us you were into each other instead of dragging it out like a damn soap opera," Jeremy muttered.

"Where's the fun in that?" Moira shot back.

Clay just smirked, putting an arm around her chair. "Took me long enough, but I get there eventually."

"Great," Kevin groaned, throwing his hands up. "Now I have to deal with a couple on top of everything else. Fantastic. Just what I needed."

"Speaking of things you need," Kirsten cut in, glaring at him, "you're still banned from talking about this whole 'Kevin's Totally Not a Zombie' podcast idea."

"Excuse me, I think the world needs to hear my story," Kevin argued. "Do you know how much I suffered?"

"You bit someone!" Moira snapped.

"Oh, please," Kevin waved her off. "Barely! I didn't even break the skin!"

"Not the point," the entire table shouted in unison.

Kevin crossed his arms, muttering, "No one ever appreciates my genius."

Fred was still here.

And, for the record, he was not happy about it.

"I helped them," he grumbled to himself, floating dramatically near the attic ceiling. "I got rid of Henry's zombieness, I made sure Kevin didn't stay undead! I kept the balance!"

From somewhere in the void, a voice muttered, "Fred, you were never supposed to be here this long."

"I'm working on it!"

"You keep saying that, yet here you are."

Fred scowled. "You think this has been fun for me?! I had to babysit two idiots, deal with an amateur summoning, and put up with Kevin. *KEVIN*. Do you know how exhausting that is?"

The void remained silent.

Fred groaned. "I need a damn vacation."

Then, with one last dramatic sigh, he vanished into the ether.

(For now.)

By lunchtime, the girls, Kevin, Henry, Joe, Jeremy, and Clay had made their way to Ruby's Diner, because what else were they supposed to do after surviving a near-apocalypse?

The diners inside had mixed reactions.

Some stared at Kevin and Henry like they still weren't sure they were really alive.

Some whispered about witchcraft under their breath.

Some just rolled their eyes and went back to their eggs and bacon like nothing had happened.

Ruby, wiping down the counter, glanced up as the group walked in.

She gave them a long, tired look.

Then she sighed, grabbed a coffee pot, and started pouring.

"Y'all want the usual?"

"Yes, please," Emmaline said.

"Extra bacon," Kevin added. "And a milkshake. And pancakes. And maybe a side of—"

"You can have *one* meal, Kevin," Kirsten cut in.

Kevin sighed dramatically. "Fine. But I'm eating all of it."

Ruby just shook her head and muttered, "I don't even wanna know."

Sheriff Dawson, now officially done with everyone's shit, refused to investigate anything supernatural ever again.

Fred was gone. ...For now.

Kevin tried to trademark the phrase "Once a Zombie, Always a Hustler."

Clay and Moira were officially dating. (About damn time.)

Joe and Jeremy still worked at the Pritchard House. ...And still thought the place was haunted.

The girls survived. ...So far.

As for Albany? It would be fine.

Eventually.

Probably.

Corvina Sweeney is a New Orleans native and cult-favorite horror author who writes from the liminal spaces where the living and the dead still linger—where something always listens. Raised near Louisiana's mist-choked bayous, she grew up surrounded by voodoo lore, forgotten tragedies, and ghost stories traded in low voices, never meant for daylight. Often called the Queen of Darkness, Sweeney is known for fully immersive, atmospheric storytelling that draws readers in gently... before refusing to let them go. Her work blurs the boundary between mystery and the macabre, allowing terror to seep slowly beneath the skin until safety feels like an illusion. A member of the prestigious Dark Veil Society—an elite circle of top indie horror authors—her stories linger long after the final page, like a bad dream that knows your name and waits for you to fall asleep.

Having Sam for Dinner

Temptress of Weinberger road

Coming Soon:

Gravemoor Radio

www.ingramcontent.com/pod-product-compliance
Lightning Source LLC
Chambersburg PA
CBHW030108310726

48970CB00004B/1196